Purple Melody

Sandra Porter

authorHOUSE®

Published by AuthorHouse 5/18/2012

ISBN: 978-1-4685-8117-1 (e)
ISBN: 978-1-4685-8118-8 (sc)

Cover design by Sandra Porter

To order copies, please contact:
AuthorHouse™
1663 Liberty Drive
Bloomington, IN 47403
www.authorhouse.com
Phone: 1-800-839-8640

www.sanporter.com

*Dedicated
to all
Saxophonists
and
Musicians*

Acknowledgments

I'm at it again, burning the midnight oil. In doing so, not a dull moment has gone by. Being most appreciative, I can't publish this book without saying thank you to those who I would like to specifically mention for their roles and for being a part of my life, spiritually and naturally.

I can never forget the Lord. Since I have engaged in writing inspirational novels, You have been my guiding light. *Thank you.*

Many thanks go out to members of my church, locally and nationally. I am grateful for the numerous supporters.

A series of shout outs, also, go out to my family and friends who, each in your own way, have been very supportive. Your focus on this project has been encouraging.

I can't continue this acknowledgment without extending my thanks to a dear cousin, Jerusha Kelson. Your timely humor that my outdated computer can no longer serve my purpose has, without a doubt, played a significant part toward completion. Your comical advice still hits a funny bone when I need a laugh or two.

And to Gail Kelson, how can I ever forget such a humble friend? I've never forgotten our sister-to-sister chat years ago. More than you know, you were an inspiration.

Once again, I wish to extend my appreciation to Windy Goodloe as editor. Pushing to stay on target was important, and I cannot say "thank you" enough for your expertise and for the long hours you have committed to this project until its completion.

Thanks to each author and reviewer of my book.

And last, but not least, I would like to thank all my readers, everywhere, for your support and for your interest in reading my third novel of this series – *Purple Melody*.

Enjoy the journey!

TABLE OF CONTENTS

Purple Melody

...let the beat begin...

SWEETSATION

Whose melodies are they?
They are born to bleed,
spoken keynotes,
opened wings.

Flurries of notes
accumulate like sand,
immense tunes of footprints,
swinging in the consciousness.

Sweetsations of joy
are unforgettable delights,
a deploy,
filtering in beams of light,
on reflections where they lay,
amazingly and strikingly displayed
in an array.

…sweetsations exhale sweet melodies.

Chapter 1

NAN MOTHER

No matter how many times I hear her voice, it just sounds sweeter than the day before. I just couldn't stop thinking about Jo-Jo. Her voice resonated the footprints of her life, which had compressed themselves deeply into my mind. I believed she had been born to bleed in anyone's memory. *I could just listen on and on for eternity, if I could.*

As she exhaled her lyrics, I inhaled her and the splendid things of nature. The music flowing from the stereo inside my home seemed to marinate the earth. It awakened the trees, causing them to react to the joyful sounds. Deeply rooted in the Georgia soil, their enormous size appeared to sway in rhythm, silently whispering their approval.

The rest of the well-established, Southern neighborhood was quiet. It was as though a shroud covered their presence and population. Everything else was so still as I gazed at the colors of nature. They had blended together and created one fascinating piece of art. The music sealed it all with the glaze of its serenity. Absorbing the arrays and etchings were like inhaling a sweet-smelling scent.

The space on the front porch had been saturated with pleasantries as my rocking chair rocked back and forth with me in it. It seemed to be just as happy. I reckoned old Liza had to keep them joints moving, just like I did.

Even though I was retired, I was still getting around, but just at a slower pace. And that was all right, because my mind was still healthy and sharp. Not bad for an almond-skin lady with long gray hair as my crown. Always have had the mark of ambition, and it still surged, every now and again, to the forefront of my spunky brown eyes. After all these years, the mark continued to run through my veins, but I, at times, had ignored the urge to exercise that side of my personality. Now, I enjoyed my leisure time and was content to mosey along for the rest of life's journey. "I'm getting younger," I said out loud and chuckled. Then, at the perfect moment, I was ready to chime in with that angelic voice as she continued to sing, "*...you will see eyes...of the melody...*"

The music kept playing, but my attention was, immediately, drawn elsewhere when, out of nowhere, a truck came to a commanding halt. Then, it rolled up in the driveway and parked.

My chair Liza and I stopped rocking to the music. I didn't need glasses to see those large letters displayed across the side of the vehicle. They were just as colorful as the radiant roses and flowers that were spread across my yard.

"It's Fed-Ex," I mumbled. Puzzled, I stared at the colorful truck. "I wonder what blew them my way this time. It must be good..."

I stood up and continued to look at the truck curiously because I wasn't expecting any deliveries. Something about the interruption had electrified the moment. On second thought, I had a feeling I would need my glasses after all to sign for whatever he had. I opened the glass door and walked through the entryway. I knew exactly where I had lain my glasses last, so I picked them up from off the table. Then, I went back outdoors to greet whoever had stolen my attention.

After several seconds, a young man, in a spiffy uniform, walked up the walkway. He carried a tube package in his hand, which made me even more curious.

Never seen him before, I thought, but he reminded me of my best friend Mr. J. They both had a mocha pigment to their skin. He was, also, smooth and satiny with thick eyebrows and chestnut brown eyes. He seemed to be the same height as Mr. J and was well built. They had similarities that just could not be ignored.

Those kinds of friends were hard to come by. I knew I would have those memories forever in the jewel box of my own heart.

"Good morning, ma'am," the courier smiled.

I stepped forward, smiled, and cordially returned the greeting as I said, "Good morning, young man. Something for me?" Full of curiosity and wonder, I thought, *What could this possibly be, and who could it be from?*

"This is for Dr. Johnston." He read the name on the label, checking for verification.

"Yes, that would be me." I said. Then, I signed for it.

Afterwards, he handed the odd-shaped package to me, "Here you are, ma'am." He paused a moment. Then, he said, "Sounds like Jo-Jo coming from inside."

I gazed up at him, surprised, and answered, "Yes, it is."

Looking at the way his eyes danced as he listened to her, it certainly was obvious that the music greeted his ears with pleasure. It amazed me that those words had come from this stranger, who I would never have thought would have been interested in this world of music, but how could anyone not? It was a soulful classic.

"You listen to her music, too?" I had to ask.

He didn't hesitate to say, "Yes, ma'am. She's one of my favorites. I like the oldies. As a matter-of-fact, I rate her number one."

With approval, I nodded and smiled again. "And…so do I."

"She's one of those icons that linger in your sleep," he added.

I slightly laughed at his comment. "I know what you mean, dear."

"Wish I could listen to more, but I must be on my way. You have a wonderful day, Dr. Johnston," he nodded with respect, revealing a dimple on one of his cheeks. It highlighted the youthfulness of his features and character.

I glanced up at him as he turned to leave and, while still holding the mystery in my hand, said, "Thank you. I will. You have a wonderful day, too."

Still smiling, I opened the glass door and walked inside to, once again, capture every word of that dynamic and beautiful voice coming from the stereo. Just when I thought I would be able to analyze what I held in my hands, I heard a horn blowing.

I put the triangular tube down in a corner in another room. I knew the package would have to wait until later. As I passed the stereo, I turned it off. I walked back to the front entrance. When I looked out, I saw my darlings getting out of the car. I opened the door and stood on the patio. I was so glad to see them.

They both rushed in my direction. Their smiles glowed like a perfect sunshine-filled day. Their mother Marcella opened her car door, too, and got out.

"Hello, Nan Mother," she yelled from the car.

"Hello, dear," I responded.

"I'll see you later today."

I waved, "All right, Marcella."

Time had flown by so quickly. Their planned visit had increased my anticipation long before the day had opened its eyes to welcome humanity.

I took a few steps and, with welcoming arms, greeted my charming teenage great-grandchildren. "Here are my two special ones."

"Buenos días, Nan Mother," said Josie, dressed in a turquoise two-piece skirt and top that reminded me of a Native American costume. Her Nestle Quik complexion blended perfectly with her charming accessories and her dark-brown hair that spiraled to her shoulders in waves.

"Good morning to you, too." I looked into her happy brown eyes. She and Jay were nearly the same complexion, but his eyes were lighter.

"Nan Mother," Jay exclaimed as he hugged me.

I exchanged the same greeting. Then, I said, "Oooooh." I could barely laugh. "You have a tight bear hug on Nan Mother this morning!"

If my back ever needed an alignment, I certainly would have known who to call. When it came to Jay, there was no escape. His hugs were among the strongest bear grips I'd ever encountered.

Josie saved me by saying, "Jay! Let Nan Mother go!" She was amused, watching him clown. He'd always had a playful spirit.

When he did let go, he pretended to catch me in case I lost my balance. He would not have had any problems with that. He was 5'11" tall and had a thick build and broad shoulders. At sixteen, he was a healthy teenager who maintained his weight well. He was a lovely youngster, who was growing into a fine, young man who was doing very well academically.

And Josie wasn't lacking any ingredients for becoming a remarkable young lady herself. For the past year, she had been mistaken to be older than her age. And I could understand why. Her maturity level was on a faster rise than most her age. Plus, her appearance and physique revealed that of a young lady. She was bright, smart, and did exceptionally well in school. Their parents had always inspired and encouraged them since they were very young. And I was their back-up support and enforcer, enlightening them to be all that they could be.

Another voice filtered into the spirit of our laughter. "Jay," the energized youngster shouted and waved as he ran across the lawn. "How you doing, man?"

Jay grinned, staring at the tall fella. "Fine, cub!"

"Ladies," he smiled at Josie and me, then dropped his football. And, in a flash, the twelve-year-old tackled Jay as if the Super Bowl depended on his defense. "I saw that!" he cackled. Overnight, he had sprung up and was, now, almost just as tall as Jay. Looked to be about 5'10" tall. He had fair skin with light-brown eyes and thick eyebrows. An undeveloped mustache could be seen, trying to yield from waaaay back behind his baby face.

"You saw...what?" Jay asked as he gasped for eternal breath.

"What were you doing to Nan Mother?"

We laughed, but the two opponents laughed even harder as they scuffled. Jay's morning had started off with a bang. He hadn't been there for more than three minutes before being ambushed. He had always enjoyed the spirit that came from that boy. The old saying was that everyone had a twin, but I thought, *There couldn't possibly be another De somewhere on this planet.* He could tickle anybody's dry bones.

"Well," I said, "I hear Jo-Jo calling."

They immediately stopped. From their reaction, they had already lost the championship.

"You do?" asked Jay.

The young boy appeared to be confused, too. "I don't hear a thing, Nan Mother."

"Josie," I said, looking at her, chuckling, and gesturing for her to go inside the house, "light up that stereo again for me and show them what Jo-Jo can do."

They grinned widely since they knew what was coming next.

Josie walked inside to play another one of her songs.

I sat down in the rocking chair, again, and rocked to the music.

Right where the youngsters were on the nicely cut green lawn, they sang background along with Jo-Jo as Josie came back outdoors to join us.

I stopped rocking and watched their demonstration.

They stared at Josie, and she knew what that meant. If she hadn't, they would have drafted her anyway. And she wasn't properly dressed to be tackled.

At first, hesitation would not let her move, but, I guessed, when she realized that there would be two against one, she probably had second thoughts. She joined them and blended in.

Impressed, I thoroughly enjoyed the spectacle. Didn't know the young fellas had it in them. I couldn't believe my receptors. Not only were they moving in unison, but they were harmonizing, too. *Had they been practicing this skit?* I wondered. The two boys were stepping like soldiers. Josie's talent, on the other hand, came as no surprise. She imitated Jo-Jo perfectly—gracefully but meaningfully.

I couldn't help but stand-up as a tear rolled down the side of my face. Mesmerized, I moved slowly to the edge of the steps. Those youngsters were full of life, giving all they had. Not long ago, they were so playful. Now, they were very serious, but, at the same time, were able to enjoy their time together. It was a good thing the sun wasn't blistering because they would've been drenched. Standing under the shade, I enjoyed every minute.

For a moment, I reminisced, visualizing Jo-Jo as she emerged. Her pinned-up hair crowned her olive face. I could see her eyes, now, set on some horizon in her distant thought, somewhere serene. A statue of a beautiful queen. The melodies in her life belonged to her...spoken keynotes. They were opened wings, soaring in flight, flying deep down in her soul. So many flurries to remember that, over time, had accumulated like sand. They were immense, often swinging in my consciousness. Sweetsations of joy were revisited, the sweetest voice during that era.

My thoughts vanished when I heard a clash of voices and laughter. It was my neighbors, the Collingsworths. Not sure how much they had seen. From their reaction, they were amused to see such a performance coming from these youngsters right here on my land.

I walked out onto the walkway.

They waved. "Good morning, Dr. Johnston," they said in unison from a distance but, not far enough away that, as a lovely couple, they did not penetrate through the picturesque scenery. Both were tall. She was slender, and he was average weight and clean-cut. His charm seeped and blended through the buttermilk of his face. She was…a complete joy.

Shifting my focus to return the greeting, I raised one arm to wave back and said, "Good morning to you both. I have been entertained graciously by your son and my great-grandchildren today." My eyes fell on them again. I had been drawn by their energy.

"I see," Nancy, his wife, stated.

Her husband, Larry, shook his head, grinning, with his hands in the pockets of his trousers. They came across the lawn to join me. They were delightful neighbors and had been living next door for some years, even before the birth of their son. They were a welcomed addition to the family, always caring and watching out for me.

Absolutely baffled, I told the Collingsworths, "I didn't know that your son De could sing."

The three entertainers completed their mission and bowed, then, hurriedly kissed me on the jaw.

Jay and De immediately erupted into laughter, somehow drawn back into their playful mood, again, as if nothing ever happened.

…how sweet the sound…

BABY GRAND

Keyboards are unique,
an art,
designed to create,
critique,
and manipulate tones,
soft or loud,
like tornadoes or clouds,
raining on the imagination.

The art is to master,
chords of variation,
unraveling formulas,
into formation,
its story,
its undertone,
which groans,
deep in the marrow of its bones.

When birthed,
it's aged but new,
the aftereffects
at its best,
free in striation,
lasting throughout its lifetime,
revealing some compelling revelations.

…some compilations are just breathtaking.

Chapter 2

CAMILLE

My trip to Atlanta turned out to be one of the best—superb weather all the way into Georgia from LAX International Airport. There had been no turbulence flying across the skies. Smooth take offs and smooth landings didn't happen every time, and I was grateful to have had both in the same day. Good weather and a good flight were just two ingredients that made the trip worthwhile. I wouldn't have changed anything.

The Southland had always captured my attention and had left a good impression on me. No matter how many times I returned to Georgia soil, the vegetation always stood out, highlighting the green of Mother Nature. What laid beyond the hardwoods was a mystery. It certainly wasn't a boring place. Southern-style homes were the stamp of its culture, which laminated clearly in my mind. They were built on level or hilly streets and winding roads. One street led to others and, oftentimes, turned into a maze. Atlanta's geography could easily be considered the capital for twisters. It took patience and a keen navigation sense. One big puzzle with many mysteries. And the cultural and historical museums, festivals, races for various causes, and historical colleges were worth the adventure, along with all the other fascinating attractions. Even the churches were pleasant to observe. Most were phenomenal. And there were a great number of them. Too many to count.

Attractions in this place were unlimited. After exiting Interstate 285 South onto Camp Creek Parkway in East Point, a conglomerate of stores and eateries stood out like flashing green lights. It was a sure way to draw customers— store after store, eatery after eatery. Should a vacationer need anything, the strip had just about every commodity or service available, including a nice place to lodge. Noteworthy hotels were among the clusters.

My stopping point was the Hampton Inn & Suites. As I walked into the immaculate and bright atmosphere, the decorative and architectural view welcomed me with opened arms. On such a pleasant day, the art of the interior design, which complimented this environment, was calming and relaxing. As soon as my eyes roamed to the right, I, while observing more of the floor plan and the décor that adorned it, saw those I had come to meet. The drawing power from their excitement caught my attention.

I smiled and greeted the attendant at the counter and walked on into the masterfully decorated lounge. The attendant realized that the waiting visitors were not strangers from their immediate outburst of cheerful and reverberating echoes.

Kathy smiled. Then, she stood and said, with open arms, "Camille!"

"Kathy!" The word ecstatically tumbled from my mouth. "How have you been? It's been a while since we've gotten together."

"I'm fine," she replied.

Glad to be amongst friends, I, then, turned toward the next person and asked emphatically, "Is that you, Paula?"

"It's me," she responded, tickled that I had even noticed that there was something different about her. She spread her arms for me to get a good look at how well she had trimmed down. She looked vibrant and had a sassy new style. Her lovely hair laid cuddly close to her Hershey brown complexion and bright, wide eyes.

"Doesn't she look great?" Kathy asked enthusiastically.

I glanced back at Kathy. "Yes, and so do you." Her silky rich hair bounced with every movement she made. "Very complimentary. I love it," I flattered her, patting her fabulous bob that surrounded her even skin tone and soft features. At nearly 5'9" tall, she had always had a slim figure.

They both were sporting new looks, dressed in colorful and dramatic clothing. Perfect. They blended in very well with the colorful environment.

Both ladies turned toward me as if they had been paid to do an initial inspection.

"You still look lovely, Camille," were Kathy's kind words. "Always smiling."

"Beautiful on the inside, as well as her outer appearance," Paula didn't hesitate to say while gesturing with her neatly manicured hands that we should all sit down.

"Thank you, ladies," I replied bubbly. There were enough compliments to go around.

I took the purse strap off my shoulder and sat with them in one of the four high-backed cushion chairs with a round table in the center. Two tall plants enclosed the little cove, giving us more privacy and separation from the other little conversation pits. Trying not to get distracted, I admired what I saw and said, "This is a very nice hotel."

The expressions on their faces had question marks all over them, as if they had forgotten to take note of their surroundings in detail. The area stood out. I definitely had walked into an unfamiliar place. The only other sound in the lounge came from a flat screen television, sitting high on a wooden shelf. Just as bright as our presence, we were surrounded by dramatic and soft tones of brown, gold, tan, green, and blue. Brown and tan couches had been placed along the wall in front of three large windows dressed with sheer drape panels. In front of the couches were matching tables and chairs. Like a catwalk extending down the center of the room was a long and high ceramic-top table with twelve high-backed stools. Long-stemmed lights hung from the ceiling. It appeared to be the main feature of the area, seemingly pointing toward the back. The dining area was vacant and in sleep mode since breakfast hours were over.

After rapidly scoping and admiring the perimeter, we were drawn into another phase of discussion. We conversed a few minutes until Nancy finally walked in and filled the only chair that had been empty. She came in glowing and bringing plenty of sunshine. We had showered her with welcoming greetings, too, as soon as she entered. Like old times, we were all together again. Since we had gone our separate ways, we had stayed in contact. We had been long overdue to join forces from across the miles.

"I know I'm running a little late, but De and our neighbors put on a little show for us this morning." She was breathing with ecstatic joy as she put her hand across her upper chest as if to stabilize her racing heart. It wouldn't have mattered if she had come early or late. As we let her know, we were just glad to see her. Normally, she had a way about her that flowed with tablespoons of grace and calm. Even though she appeared a little hyper, the background of her personality still took control. Her own unique attributes seeped through the walls of her mannerisms. She had never changed and had developed into a wise and intelligent lady who sought and capitalized on being better than she was the day before. Her outlook on life made all the greenery of her being sprout into fruition. As a professor of psychology, she took her career and spiritual energy seriously and showed no lack of just pure soul-searching. Maybe that was what had drawn her husband, Larry, to her.

Likewise, Kathy and Paula capitalized on the paths they had chosen. Kathy, a pediatrician, loved children and was full of vitality and warmth. After her visit to Africa, her conviction and commitment to service had risen to higher heights. She had seen the hurting drill of sorrow at its best, which had dug deep holes of diseases and sickness into a poor population.

"A fierce shadow of delusional suffocation left a purple and black overcast," which, in her words, described the scene. In that part of the hemisphere, it was looming and dark. Although medical aid had come, especially in developing countries, there was never enough. That experience was an eye-opener, and it made Kathy treasure her career that much more. If there was only one song that she could sing that would help dissipate any fierce shadow, that song would be sung out of an act of love. Love had everything to do with it. The medical field had allowed her to tap into an even broader scope of suturing the ills of humanity. She realized that her purpose and contribution were greatly needed. The inscription of her character was to be desired, which was her own unique calligraphy. Her signature was about care and concern. Entering into the medical field was one of the best things that could have ever happened to her.

And Paula, a lawyer, who had outlawed supremacy of character within herself, also, had an interesting signature. She had been her prime case study and had adamantly refrained from falsely staging the person she had not been created to be. She was her own advocate. Her feeling about getting the most out of divine humanity was to be kind and real. She had witnessed a lot that could have either pawned her into ruthlessness or, preferably, prepared her to be better in a cruel world. Exponentially, she felt that an occupation should only be worn in its place—humbly, in the silence of the heart. Her motto was "The heart is where matters are dealt with and resolved, in the interim, to bring out the best in an individual". In doing so, she refused to sabotage herself. She only liked sweet icing on a well-rounded cake. Her cheery personality and drive had helped others along the way during her journey and had made a difference in society. And, maybe, that was what had drawn Paula and Kathy's husbands to them.

At the turn of the conversation, Paula looked in my direction, bright-eyed. "Camille, how is Jarvis? Is he still on the map?" she slightly teased.

Kathy's and Nancy's eyes beamed on me, too, so I leaned forward for complete confidentiality, even though no one else could possibly hear.

"I should say so," was my whispered but amusing remark.

My erect posture and air called to mind someone acting in the early 1900s. Not surprised, my response captured their full attention.

At first, shock was scribbled across the pads of their faces. Shortly after, spurts of laughter erupted among them. Even I had to join in because it wasn't too often the comical side surfaced beyond anything more than mild kidding.

When I zoomed into Nancy's searching and questioning eyes, she asked, puzzled, "I've been waiting to ask. What's the secret?" She remembered we hadn't finished a prior conversation we had been having not too many days ago.

As the others were jovially commenting, before I said anything, I drifted. I thought, *If I could play a baby grand, what story would I play? Or what chord would I play? Would it be dramatic or serene? How old will it get? What aftereffects could possibly be shared? What would be the revelation? Its undertone and groans are deep in the nutrients of its marrow; it's shielded in privacy. Unraveling formulas of tunes fall into formation. They sing out from the dark when they're birthed by light. But…when will it be free in striation?* Another thought trickled down— something I hadn't even thought of. *Can the birth of any tune and chord ever tell some old but new compelling revelation? How long will it age? Some are designed to be mastered…*

After refocusing, I realized that all three ladies, circled around the center table, were still waiting intently. Neither one, it seemed, had blinked. They were so still…like mannequins. Their eyes were filled with wonder.

"Camille!" Their voices rang out at the same time, bewildered, but somewhat tickled as I smiled. As long as I had paused, I couldn't blame them.

I drew in a big breath of fresh air and reached for my purse. When I looked inside, the items weren't there.

…hmmm, the tones to this beat have manipulatively dropped a few notes…

SCALE

Scales are distinctive,
along black and white keys,
with flats,
minors and sharps,
from a through g,
sounds on the musical tree.

Where on the scale
are stories defined?
From some creation,
in the midst of time.

First, the test,
finding a tune,
somewhere between,
do-re-mi,
or,
fa-sol-la-ti-do.
Sometimes, a wild guest,
up until high noon,
to solve the quest.

…on the scale lies interesting roots.

Chapter 3

NAN MOTHER

Some places are just meant to baste your thoughts. I relished the basil in which they simmered, the fragrance I delighted in wherever my mind roamed. And just at that very moment, it was no different. We had been walking the neighborhood, enjoying the stroll. Josie's idea of getting some exercise was what I had needed. Strolling, arm in arm, she made a good attendant, conversationalist, and listener. Her smiles and darling personality made the day even brighter. Her presence was enjoyable.

Routinely, I went for walks to meditate and to move my aging limbs. Afterwards, I usually felt renewed and like a youngster again. Occasionally, there would be others with the same thing in mind. But, that day, the only life being that was visible and moving with more speed than Josie and me, captured our attention, while heading our way.

"Ooooh," I chuckled. "Look who's running up the street!"

Josie was just as amused.

"Dusty! Where are you headed?" I said to one of the neighbor's pets.

His owner, Danny, wasn't far away. He shouted out one of the most popular commands for the escapee to halt.

The dog stopped, then sat in front of us. He barked, then looked behind himself.

We entertained Dusty until his owner approached with a leash in his hand.

"This dog is quick," my neighbor chuckled. "The moment he saw you, Nan Mother, he took off. Other than my mother, you're the only one he'll run to."

I looked down and smiled at the dog. "I'm glad you recognized me, Dusty. You have always watched out for me." I patted him on the head.

The fella, then, acknowledged Josie.

"How are you doing these days, dear?" I inquired.

He smiled widely and answered, "I'm doing well."

"Good."

"I don't need to ask you that question, Nan Mother. You look great."

"Do I?"

Josie was tickled. "Yes, Nan Mother," she said, reassuring me without hesitation.

Dusty barked. The sudden interruption warranted our attention.

"Oh, you think so, too, huh?" were my exact words.

Danny laughed and said, "Well, someone else agrees with me."

"Well, I'm convinced."

He snapped the leash onto Dusty's collar. "Well, Nan Mother, we have to move along. I have some errands to run. My relatives, Kenny and Ronnie, are waiting for me."

"I certainly understand. You take care of yourself. Come by and see Nan Mother sometimes."

He smiled, "I will, and take care, Josie."

She said good-bye and bid her farewells to Dusty, too, as he and his owner turned and trotted back home. She locked her arm around mine, again, and held on like a bodyguard.

"Dusty is funny, Nan Mother."

I patted the back of her youthful hand and responded, "Dear, I have to agree with you." I looked up at the roof of the earth and inhaled deeply to exercise my lungs. The air felt clean and crisp. After the paired organs expanded to their fullest capacity, I exhaled. "I care for that young man. He's very friendly, and he's always there if anyone ever needs his help. And he has the jolliest laugh I've ever heard. My only complaint is that I just don't hear it enough."

My attendant just listened.

"And, great-granddaughter, I care about you, too."

She smiled. "I know you do, Nan Mother."

Immediately, I added, "I am so proud of you and Jay. You've done so well in school, and I hope you continue to do your best. You are in high school now, and subjects may get tougher. I hope you know that you have plenty of help in your corner." I glanced at her.

Josie looked at the ground. She seemed to be counting our footsteps. "Yes, ma'am," was her response.

"This will be the last stage before entering into college. Are you still planning to become a teacher?"

It didn't take her long to answer. She replied, "Not anymore."

"Oh, no?" I didn't hesitate to say. She certainly piqued my curiosity.

She shook her head.

Surprised by her response, I projected, with emphasis, "No? Then…what?"

Ever since she was a young girl, she had always wanted to be an educator. Nothing else had seemed to matter.

"I no longer want to be a teacher. I want to go into psychology or psychiatry."

I lit up. "Oh, my." I couldn't stop smiling.

"I'm not certain yet, but I do know those two fields interest me."

Wanting to know more, I, then, asked, "What made you change your mind? Nan Mother is just curious. It's not that I'm questioning your decision. I think it's great!" I glanced at her, waiting to hear her reason.

"Well, Nan Mother," she said, appearing to be happy that we were having this discussion, "I want to help people."

"But, why psychology or psychiatry?" I felt the need to investigate further out of a burning curiosity. "Why not internal medicine, nursing, or ophthalmology? And that's just a few, dear. There are many areas to consider."

She paused for a moment. Maybe, she hadn't thought about why psychology had hit the top of her list versus all the other options she could have chosen. "Psychology is intriguing. I want to know what ails the mind, and I want to help people who have disorders, so they can have a better quality of life. Making a contribution toward good mental health is, I feel, important."

I welcomed her decision and could only smile, reminding myself that my great-grandchild was growing up. It seemed like only yesterday she was crawling on her knees from room to room. In the past, I had traveled often, visiting other states. In various locations, I would purchase her the cutest little dresses with matching bows. And I couldn't leave without something for her feet. Doll shoes were treasure hunts. They were so precious. I always brought back something for her and Jay. They both had stolen my heart. And now...she looked at me, eye to eye, and made her own decisions. So grown up.

Gazing at her again, I told her, "Mental disorders are crippling. Society does need your help, too. I'm glad that you have taken into consideration those options. I, specifically, like your answers on why you would like to enter into either profession."

She held on tighter, maybe feeling more secure. "I hoped that you would approve, Nan Mother."

"Honey, you don't need my approval. I am confident that, whatever decision you make, it will be a good one. It is your career; you must run with it, like you have found a treasure of gold—"

Josie interjected with laughter, then comically said, "Without the pirates, right, Nan Mother?"

Tickled, I patted the back of her hand, again, and, while nodding, replied, "Yes, without the pirates." Then, something else dawned on me. "It's still a little early, but have you thought about what college you would like to attend?"

"I have," she said without delay. "I would like to attend Spelman College."

"That's a good choice. Nan Mother attended Spelman College."

Her eyes widened as she gazed at me. "You did?" I knew she would be ecstatic.

I nodded. "Yes, I did. Decades ago. That college has a lot of history behind it."

"I've read snippets about it," Josie said excitedly.

To give her a little background on what she may or may not know, I said, "Spelman College is a liberal arts school and has been around for a long time, since 1881—"

She interjected once more, "That's a long time."

"Years of memories for so many alumnae. There's a lot I will share with you later, but just remember…if you need to seek counseling, for whatever reason, do not wait until there's a crisis. If you have the chance to visit the campus anytime in the near future, stop by and introduce yourself to Dr. Ave Marshall. She's a very nice and helpful lady."

Wondering, she asked, "Is she the only one who works in that office?"

"Oh, no. As far as I know, she has a staff of seven plus an intern or two. I'm almost certain that Dr. Vickie Ogunlade, Merrine McDonald and Pamela Jenkins are still there. I'm sure they would be of help, also. Besides those mentioned, a psychiatrist is there a couple of days or more each month. They offer a wide range of services and provide all the help a student would need. Phenomenal staff."

She promised by saying, "I will, and I won't forget. Scout's honor!"

I hadn't heard those last two words in a long time, but I knew she meant it. Rarely did she make commitments she could not keep.

Since we were on the topic of school, something else surfaced. I now thought about Jay, so I said, "I wonder if your brother still has plans on attending Morehouse College."

"We had that conversation not long ago," she let me know. "That is his plan. If not, then Howard University or Harvard are his other choices."

"Great selections. However, if he knew who Dr. Benjamin E. Mays was…"

Distracted, I heard a familiar noise. The sound reminded me of Fed-Ex. I turned around. Didn't see a truck anywhere. That strange package that had been delivered to me that morning had begun to radiate in my mind. Oddly, I didn't know who had sent it. *What on earth could that be?* was the question I kept asking myself, over and over, again. *Who sent it?* These thoughts continually stood out at the forefront, blocking everything else I wanted to say on the current topic matter. It reminded me of auditions, trying to pass the test to sing with the choirgirls. Never failed, but, I had certainly got lost while trying to find a tune befitting for the situation. There was only one musical tree for so many scenarios. And, in this case, I wouldn't have been able to even hum the musical scale out of pure bewilderment. So far, there was no connection to that package to even camouflage by pantomiming. This quest, I guessed, wouldn't be solved until high noon, exactly the time when all my questions were answered.

Josie asked, "What is it, Nan Mother?"

I slowly turned back around, facing the path ahead of us. "Humph," I responded, puzzled. "Something a little strange happened this morning before your mother dropped you and Jay off at the house."

Her eyebrows furrowed. "Strange?" She stared at me as she waited for more information.

"Yes," I pondered, "Fed-Ex came by this morning. I wasn't expecting anything. And what's so strange is that I don't recognize the sender. An odd package out of the blue would cause anyone to wonder."

"I know I would."

"When I get back to the house, I'll have to open it."

When the last word trailed from my mouth, Josie stopped and grinned with a very bright smile. Her sudden reaction caused that package to disappear from my mind. She pointed, as we were about to walk past a black truck parked on the street in front of the next door neighbor's house. As we stared into its dark black-tinted windows, we saw that our reflections were crystal clear. The vehicle shone and sparkled like a mirror, hanging on a wall, low enough for me to get a good look at myself. Although the sun beamed down throughout the community, there was plenty of shade. Trees serenely hovered near my end of the neighborhood.

Where we stood, I was captured by a sudden breeze. Swiftly, it came through and lightly fanned the bottom of my dress. It brought with it the fragrance of flowers, which trailed up the cavities of my nostrils.

Josie placed her hand on top of her head before her hat flew off. As an added measure of security, a set of strings that hung from the sides had been tied into a knot. Even if it flew off, it wasn't going anywhere other than dangling from the base of her neck. It reminded me of those western cowgirl hats. What other kind of headwear would be better suited for riding horses and escaping the Comanche and other

Native American posses, while galloping at high speed? As for me, my headpiece fitted securely down over my crown. It shielded my face from direct sunlight, a modern-day brim neatly woven but sturdy. We were two ladies, sporting two very different styles, who were trying to be photogenic for an image that would be held only in our memories.

I couldn't help but gingerly join Josie in her girly amusement. We were enjoying our time together. These kinds of moments were just too special to go by unnoticed. Our reflections were rich through the lens of my eyes. The exposure gleamed. It felt as though I had been examining a picture through my glasses that gave me the highest resolution possible.

"I like your sombrero. Would you like to trade?" She smiled at our doubles.

Once again, impressed with her Spanish skills, I answered, "Why not? I like yours, too!"

She purely giggled.

Jovially, I added, "I must go where you shop, dear. It is one of a kind."

Without any lost words, her response was, "With all the lovely hats that you have, Nan Mother, I should tag along with you to your secret hideouts. When you go to church services, you dress like you are going to a serious photo shoot."

Her comment caused me to gasp with laughter.

Taking full advantage of this opportunity, Josie purposely posed, leaning her head to touch mine as if she was preparing herself for a snapshot on the perfect day.

Then, I told her, "Dear, we must keep walking before the neighbors begin to wonder why we are facing their visitor's vehicle."

Moving on, she agreed.

As we got closer to the property lines of my home, we could see that what was up ahead held no dull moments.

Jay and De were still at it on the lawn. They were playing football, tackling, and throwing the ball. Even if just the two were playing, they always had some excitement going. If they never had an audience, they could always count on one watching from the sideline. And that was Midnight, De's dog, who was as big as a black, rocky mountain. That was what I called him. The interesting breed—My golly!—looked solid as a rock with muscles rippling from his mountainous body. According to De, he was only six months old and already a big fella. I wouldn't want to ever be on his dinner plate. Looked like he couldn't wait to jump in, hind legs and all. And no sooner had the thought emerged, when the ball went flying high in the air. That dog's head and eyes went up, too, waiting to see where it would land, I supposed. And when it did, all I heard was a clash of voices. I guessed those boys had tumbled down somewhere between the tree line.

Like most dogs, Midnight's mind was steady ticking. The ball slid to the edge of the yard. At that moment and at an opportune time, all he could see were flashing green lights. Not far from his feet was where it laid. He ran, gripped the ball with his teeth, and took off.

I could clearly see what was taking place now with the boys. That clever dog gave them some of his own entertainment, dodging and running circles around Jay.

De lunged toward him.

Midnight ran quickly behind him, then animatedly ran circles around Jay again.

Josie laughed.

"Did you see that?" I said. "He's quick!"

"I did," she nodded, astonished. "Now, that's football!"

"It certainly is."

Two cars passed by. I recognized one vehicle, which Nancy drove. She parked it in her driveway. The other vehicle parked in front of her house.

In the meantime, the opponents were still at it, trying to catch the thief who had boldly confiscated the ball. So far, Midnight seemed to have scored all the points. He let the ball drop from his mouth momentarily and got a breather or two in. Before long, they ganged up on him on both sides. That dog had eyes on the front and back of his body as he calculated his next move. Quickly, the boys rushed him. Jay was only able to touch the lower part of his back, but Midnight somehow slipped through the cracks of their failed plan and flew next door.

"Mom!" De pointed at the runaway as she got out the car. "Stop him!"

…the beat is getting interesting…

MUSIC

Composition of music has structure,
a science or art of combining tunes
and tones,
a continuity in the making,
of its new profound home.

Added vocal or instrumental sounds
are additions to its homeland,
having harmony,
melody,
or rhythm,
craftily measured into its woven,
elegant crown,
with ornaments,
decked all around.

Melodies are sweet,
agreeable sounds,
speeding up,
slowing it down,
flurries of beats,
filtering softly,
like sifted wheat,
in the heart,
where fireplaces burn,
unveiling the part.

…music is played and defined from its birthplace.

Chapter 4

CAMILLE

So much laughter filled the air. Five ladies were having a merry time out on the back lawn where an abundance of greenery enhanced the relaxed atmosphere. At the moment, I listened. Before I realized it, my mind had wondered off and gazed the premises. I was impressed. The lawn was perfectly cut, which suited the foundation that set the stage. Trees and foliages added life to the property. It all blended so perfectly, as if each had been specifically etched with a stencil, then freshly colored by nature. Just enough bright seasonal flowers were planted around the gazebo. Noticeably, someone had taken the time to use their imagination in detailing the property. It could've equaled the best of fine arts. It was picture perfect. We were happily surrounded by the pleasantries of this site in living color.

Appearance was everything. Being in the right place at the right time gave me the serenity that I needed before the day ended. Given a good dose of mental therapy gelled my mood; the miniature pond nearby made it just that much more therapeutic. The waterfall sounded like a musical rainfall, as droplets splashed with yellow rosebuds floating in no certain direction. They seemed so calm, slowly moving along with grace. Their appearance and effects blended in with the design of nature and all the conversation that was taking place. Recaptured by the festive atmosphere, I smiled as the young lady approached with a pitcher of lemonade. Soon after, she brought a colorful tray with matching tall plastic glasses filled with ice. She poured lemonade in each, then handed me one.

"Thank you," I said to her, smiling.

"You're welcome."

She came back with a platter of cookies, then sat with us. She took a seat next to the precious lady who had welcomed us into her home. When we saw the big black dog with a football in its mouth heading in our direction when we drove into Nancy's driveway, this striking lady was humored. No one, other than Nancy, had gotten out of the car until Midnight was gone from sight. Kathy and Paula hadn't moved in the other vehicle. This was how we all met Dr. Johnston, who joined in with Nancy and told us we had nothing to fear. And this was when she invited us to join her, drawing us in with pure and sunshiny delight.

Some things were just meant to shine where whispers of revelations could not be dismissed. Just as I had thought, first impressions usually carried the most weight. From the moment I had seen Dr. Johnston, she had a rare gift for captivating those she came in contact with. Her spirit danced all around us with welcoming arms. Salve from her presence was timely and needed. Her smiles and darling personality came in the right dosage. With charm, charisma, and warmth, her makeup constituted the song of her natural being.

And Josie was so adorable. I just had to ask at the opportune time, "Sunshine, what are your aspirations? I have a feeling you are on a mission." I smiled at the womanly young girl who hosted us as if she had done this many times before. Her persona led me to believe that she would someday take charge of her destiny and do great things.

She glanced at her great-grandmother with the biggest smile. Then, she looked at me and said, "A psychologist or psychiatrist."

"I'm impressed." I gave my grin of approval.

As calm and tactful as Nancy usually was, her reaction went up another notch. "I'm impressed, too. I never knew that. I'm a professor of psychology. We have to talk." Nancy gazed at her with great surprise, and it showed from the excitement in her voice. She pulled out a business card from her caddy and handed it to her.

Josie scanned the card and welcomed the invitation with a twinkle in her smile. "Thank you. I would love that." Her excitement became transparent. She probably didn't know she had a mentor right in their back yard, the perfect candidate for her to shadow in her field of interest.

Dr. Johnston beamed. "It's a coincidence that you asked, Camille. Josie and I just had this same conversation earlier today. I think she will do very well."

In agreement, I replied, "And so do I, Dr. Johnston."

"My dear, just call me Nan Mother. That's what everyone else calls me in the neighborhood. We're family… all family."

Kathy and Paula picked up their glasses just as I did and nodded.

"That's really great, Josie," Kathy encouraged her more with Paula agreeing, too.

"As you continue to turn pages in your life, the melody of your destiny should sound sweeter and sweeter," I added.

Paula assured her, "You have some backing and backup and some more. You have…" she paused to count everyone present, "five in your corner."

Nan Mother sweetly cut in to say, "She has six."

Before she could say another word, music engulfed the air.

Josie chuckled, looking toward the glass sliding door.

We followed her gaze.

Jay slid the patio door open with a glass in his hand. "Nan Mother, I knew before long you were going to ask Josie to turn on Jo-Jo again." He grinned.

She appeared tickled that he knew what she had in mind to do. She agreed, "You're absolutely right, dear. Thank you."

"You're welcome." He slid the door back and disappeared.

Somehow, I hadn't noticed the outdoor speakers. They were camouflaged in the setting with all the other colorful arrays. What I began to hear beating against the platform of my eardrums had my attention. *Who is that?* I wondered. Didn't recall ever hearing her voice before.

Nan Mother set her glass down and politely said, "Excuse me, ladies." She stood up from her chair at the end of the lawn table. "I will return shortly."

We acknowledged her departure as she turned and headed for the glass sliding door.

"And I'll bring some water and more cookies," Josie said as she slid the door open for her. When they both disappeared inside, the conversation shifted until they returned.

There were times when some things just couldn't wait, and it showed on the others' faces. The subject of the missing envelopes was at the top of their list. After realizing that they were in my travel bag once we left the This Is It restaurant across from the hotel, I handed one to each of them. The topic matter had been put on hold. No matter how many times the subject came up, cell phones were ringing without relief. Calls kept coming. Timing was everything, and this was a good opportunity to pick up where we had left off when Kathy leaned forward to begin the fireside chat.

Since I had ridden with Nancy, I had already filled her in along the way. However, she leaned in, too, to join in what seemed like the most private conversation ever between the four of us.

"This is great," Kathy smiled at me. "Does Jarvis know?"

Music, which had captivated my undivided attention along with the sound effects of the waterfall, grew louder from the silence. From the gazes, they were intrigued by the appetizer and were waiting for the full-course meal to be served, so that all their questions would be answered. Their anticipation swelled as we engaged further in the conversation.

Before long, behind us, we heard the glass sliding door open. "Oh, yes! Now, where were we?" Nan Mother asked in the kindest voice, while headed back to her seat.

We all sat back, welcoming the sunshine of this lady. We were ready to recapture the prior topic, which had left us all in suspense. Just as I did, everyone else realized that there were only five of us around the table, plus one teenager. *Who could she possibly be referring to?*

"You were responding to Paula's statement when she said I have backing, and backup and some more. She said five, and you said six," Josie reminded her, word for word.

Nan Mother sat down. "Yes, I remember that," she nodded her head. "Listen…"

It was quiet. That voice streaming from the speakers sounded rich and profound. Although I didn't recognize the songstress, her mesmerizing abilities reminded me of someone I knew. Someone who, also, had his composition of music marked to a science. I often wondered how he could weave notes and tones into such an elegant crown of music. In the right dosages, he knew how to measure exactly the right amount of harmony and rhythm. It was his homeland where he sang music from deep down inside the fireplace of his rich heart. His blessing, for certain, ran extremely deep. *How many ornaments on a crown did this man actually have?* I wondered. From what I had witnessed, he was an all-around individual, decked with the best. Audiences were always engaged in the flurries of his beats. And the dressings of his lyrics took them back home, filtering down like sifted wheat. I had to admit...all that I had heard were nothing but agreeable sounds. At that moment, I reflected on one of his performances, which seemed to blend perfectly with the music and voice that was already playing through the speakers. I smiled at the thought that the two would make a wonderful singing pair.

Nan Mother spoke again with pride and continued the conversation from where she trailed into meditation, "Jo-Jo, my dear. She is the sixth angel, the angel of words and sweet melodies."

Like most teenagers, Josie took it all in and smiled at her great-grandmother's response.

Everyone else just listened, seemingly enjoying their own time of meditation and the refreshments.

"I like her style," I said, almost at a whisper. "I know of someone who would really appreciate her music."

"Who might that be?" the lady of the house asked. Her eyes danced with anticipation just as the effects of the music did.

While staring at my glass of lemonade, I told her, "Devin Fairchild."

"Fairchild?" she repeated. Her eyes gazed upwardly. "That name is *very* familiar." She appeared a million miles away.

...tunes to this beat had drawing power...

BASS

A bass is an instrument
used to produce music,
played by an instrumentalist,
constructing a musical piece.

It's noted for its unique thunder,
the lowest pitch in range,
extremely deep,
amplifying the beat,
like the intensity of lions,
roaring on mountaintops,
growling notes of its presence,
shaving every layer of silence.

Mastered from its strings,
are mysterious pulses,
a combustion,
KABOOM!
pounding from the heat,
dramatizing,
powerful as hurricanes,
ricocheting in the plains,
erupting quakes,
to the core of the bone,
before it simmers,
have left and gone,
leaving a trail of tremors,
a lasting memory.

…when it thunders, soon comes the rain.

Chapter 5

DEVIN

Three years later, I'm back in Atlanta. Since my last visit, this geographic spot in the United States had remained photographed in my memory. Since it was one of the most eye-catching places to visit, how could I have forgotten? The landmark of the South had left its mark on me. Rightfully so, history branded this state with its own flag, miraculously staged with stars of notable men and women. During a minatory time period, so many factors had come into play. And…there were so many time frames to revisit. The cause was so drastic with each, and the measurements of the outcomes were so extensive and powerful. That flag, which flew for eternity as a reminder of its significance, wavered in one direction with a three-angle spear—parity, peace, pray. In the face of "the ages," it hung from the pole of altruism.

The thought of one of those amazing stars of notable men flashed before my eyes. Dr. Benjamin E. Mays, a warrior of his time, accomplished major tasks for social change. Even so, being a part of change had allowed many students in this country to seek their dreams. Designed to be a minister, educator, and civil rights activist, his role in life stood out like fireworks, brightly lighting up skies inside cerebellums. One man—on the grounds of Howard University and Morehouse College, as well as other places—had had so many battles, but, during most of his trying times and while riding out high tides, he scored victories. His convictions enabled him to infiltrate most of the walls of injustice that blocked his progression. Gifted, he was world renown. Determined and dynamic in his articulation as an inspiring orator and motivator, the root of his cause left no stones unturned. He was one who could not be plucked from the ground where he had been so deeply rooted in memory. *So long ago*, I further thought, *but not forgotten*. His stature was what I called unforgettable, still shining around the world because of his deeds. He was a protagonist, one of the most notable icons of his time, who had mended and expanded the arena of higher education, and the institution's physical sites right in the heart of the deep South and abroad. Compellingly, he had even mentored Dr. Martin Luther King, Jr. His duration had not been wastefully depleted.

And there was Dr. John A. Kenney, Sr., a highly skilled and devoted surgeon during the 20th century. Born in the 1800s, the whistle of his destiny blew loudly and clearly as he performed tedious and miraculous surgeries that drew widespread attention. As his prime focus, he profoundly dedicated his time to helping people who needed medical attention. Obviously, from his long list of outstanding accomplishments, his success story had put him in high rankings. Med students shadowing his expertise could not have gained any better experience than from an expert who knew his trade quite well. His knowledge and gifts set him high among his colleagues and the people who came in contact with him. His love for what he did permeated through his craft and teaching. Because of his dynamics, unfortunately, he and his family were inevitably forced to move and relocate elsewhere. Amazingly, during that era, he opened a hospital in New Jersey to service any and all that he could without duress and conning from outside parties trying to capitalize and monopolize on his dream. He had foreseen what laid ahead. Determined not to fail, he succeeded. "Incredible," I mumbled as the word seeped from my mouth in astonishment. So masterful with his skills that two of the most renowned men during that time were especially drawn to him. He was a personal physician to Booker T. Washington and George Washington Carver.

"Some deeply seeded history," I couldn't help but say. Then, I thought, *What a dynamic story written by Linda Kenney Miller. Historical footage recorded in <u>Beacon on the Hill</u> was…captivating.*

My focus on another fine print in history had stolen my immediate attention during an afterthought. *How could I ever forget the special people who have impacted my life through dreams and realities of the past and present?* Some things were just not forgotten. Maybe dormant for a season, but, when memory called, the condition of the thought would rain or snow. And my present thought drizzled with pleasure, capturing slides of my last performance there.

I couldn't resist thinking about Joy singing for Ms. PeggyAnn and the fact that Ms. PeggyAnn's friends, who anonymously requested my presence, had appeared as the feature.

"Umph," I still couldn't believe it. Never heard of or experienced what my buddy Jarvis jokingly referred to as being "nominated" to do what Joy called "do what you do best." Intrigued, the evening was something I could do all over again, including all the other mysteries that surrounded the occasion. Barricaded by suspense, I didn't know what to think. Neither did Jarvis, to some extent. No magnifying glass could have even helped unravel the small print for an analytical eye to solve. In disarray, pieces of the interesting puzzle felt like one cold trail after the other. I was trapped in a maze of confusion. As each startling piece unfolded, the clock started ticking louder and louder as time drew near for the ballerina to bow. The last piece of the clue chimed on time. When the ballerina did bow, even the twister of my own imagination sailed. So surreal. A twister that only time would reveal because I didn't have a clue. I thought, *How many of those special scenes could actually be recaptured for a remaking?* None could be reenacted or defined, other than those chosen, since the colors of time were destined, revealing its mysterious eyes. They had been mystifying throughout history. I wondered, *Had the eye been fully colored for viewing?* There was no more film left on the reel in my mind, so, I'd never know. But I would always remember that beat. Fascinated, the weekend was well spent and worth the time for a special cause.

I chuckled from a sudden thought. The scene that jet skied to the forefront had to be revisited. How often did I get a cramp in my neck and in my leg seconds apart? Never. But the truth was that it happened. It occurred when I went to church with Jarvis. At a highpoint during the devotional part of their service is when the orchestration went from a swaying to swinging. Their choir dynamically sang with a beat and rhythm that would make a flying bird faint and drop from the sky. After a while, swinging my neck and patting my feet to the speed led me to the comforts of ER in my own home. As difficult as it was to get out of Jarvis's car, I made it, limping and hopping, to a nice hot tub of water to soak in. It felt like eternal relaxation. However, the most important thing was the deliverance of the sermon. The message came right on time, and it was well worth it and some more.

And the expression I must have had on my face when Mr. Wage asked me to sing without music for a brief audition in his office. Although I passed with flying colors, the unusual request had taken me by surprise. I thought the interview would be like the other meetings I'd attended. I'd thought that I would simply provide him with a sample of one of my performances. His reaction will never be erased from my mind. He was one of a kind and one of the jolliest I'd ever met. With his approval, every note rain-dropped right on time and sealed the agreement.

It was one of those moments that I just couldn't seem to stop. The onset of memories beat real strong in my mind. Now…on to another beat of my own, I drove into Stone Mountain Park, astonished to see what lay ahead. As one of the natural wonders of the world, the unusual, but interesting site was known for its rarity. Trimmings of attractions surrounded the base of a huge granite rock with carvings of three men on horses. Each horse paraded Confederate President Jefferson Davis, Generals Robert E. Lee and Thomas "Stonewall" Jackson. Inception to completion ranged from 1912 to 1972. The sixty-year delay resulted from World War I, World War II and a few other obstacles. From miles away, the main feature stood out, resembling a mountainous dome. It was impossible to miss in flight or on land this popular feature of the antebellum South. This Confederate memorial was brought to life by laser shows during the summer nights. Incredibly detailed, now the spectacular symbolized the promise—imposing over the present carving another image: Dr. Martin Luther King, Jr.—of a New South.

Among the monumental distractions, visitors of various nationalities edited my view. A colorful distribution of ethnic groups reminded me of a fascinating abstract, some lovely painting that would be difficult to miss. The beauty and charm put into the making made it an interesting piece. I recognized how valuable it was. As I drove slowly, I glanced at the mixture of diversity that was striated against the canvas of the earth. And there was still room left on the canvas and more to come.

During the time when I was observing as much as I could on both sides of the road, the radio host announced the time, but I could barely hear the sound. Wondering about the time, I looked at the clock. It was 10:30 A.M. *Perfect timing.* Just as I looked up, I spotted relatives in the designated picnic area. I parked, then locked the car door after getting out. Soon after, I waved, acknowledging everyone from a distance, including my immediate family. It appeared they were cheerfully waiting for more to arrive, but the morning was just getting started. Normally, our reunions took place in June or July, but, this year, family members had decided to have it during the Memorial Day weekend to escape the hottest heat waves. They had made a good decision because the weather proved itself to be comfortable. So far.

Imani met me at the path. Her radiant smile always captured my heart.

"Heyyyyy, sis," I joyously said, slightly bending to hug my only sibling. I couldn't ask for a better sister and was grateful.

"Devin!"

I welcomed her firm grasp.

"I'm glad to see you," she said.

"I'm glad to see you, too, Imani."

She looked beautiful in her floral maxi dress that draped to her sandals. Very stylish. I could smell her flowery perfume; the scent wafted from her caramel pores.

The other two important people in my life were just as happy to see me. They watched as if they were viewing a nice picture that was too hard to take their eyes away from.

Imani and I strolled to where they were.

My mother extended her arms as she stepped forward to greet me. "Devin, Devin, Devin," she repeated ecstatically.

My mother ReJoyce was no taller than Imani, who was near 5'9" tall. They had the same complexion, and they looked so much alike with their poppy-brown eyes. One had shoulder length hair, and the other had very long hair.

At the sound of that, I chuckled and said, while giving her a bear hug, "Beautiful, beautiful, beautiful."

She looked up and hugged me again, tickled.

Pop jokingly chimed in to capitalize on his territory, "That's my line, son, but I guess that's all right."

My pop Lance and I were the two with the most height. We surpassed the 6-foot mark, easily. That was our trademark, branded in our genes. The skin we wore dressed it well.

"What can I say, chief?" I defended myself, cackling right along with him.

I was drawn into his sudden grasp and man-to-man pat on the back. With plenty of energy circulating, it's as though we were making up for lost time, but the past can never be recouped.

Although Mom seemed to have felt special by the remarks, she chortled, too.

In addition, I said, "She's just that. I can't blame you, Pop."

Imani smiled with approval, "She sure is."

Before he started to say something else, other relatives approached me, exchanging greetings with glee. Some I hadn't seen in a long time, and a few I didn't remember ever seeing before, but they fit and blended right in.

"So, Devin," Pop said at an opportune time after everyone had dispersed to engage in other conversations, "I hope things are still going well for you."

"Excuse me," Imani said. "I'll be back."

We acknowledged her and walked toward one of the picnic tables to sit down and catch up.

Like most mothers, Mom asked, "Yes, and how are you doing these days?" The search ran deep in her eyes. She added, "Well, since the time we talked to you last?"

We sat.

"Beautiful, it's only been about three weeks," Pop kindly interjected, grinning at her.

I coolly chuckled. Sitting on the opposite side of the table, I confirmed, "Mom, sounds like you miss me."

"I do, like most parents. Obviously, you can tell."

Sitting directly in front of me, Pop took it even further, "Devin, she talks about you often. As a matter-of-fact, we both do."

"You know, I had to ask, but, maybe, I shouldn't have because if you weren't doing so well, you would have called. You have been very good about keeping us posted."

"Yes, I would have." I couldn't deny. "Thanks for being you, Mom. I know three weeks is stretching it a little, but things are moving along nicely. No complaints. And I'm doing well."

"Good!" Pop replied.

Just what she wanted to hear, she nodded and smiled, sitting daintily in a dress similar to the one Imani had on. Sunshine flowed from the sunrise she brought with her. The rays of her being were hard to miss.

Pop, then, said, shaking his head, "It's still hard to believe we have an artist in the family. When is your next singing engagement?"

"Very soon. Between my contract with Gospel Child Record Label Company and Jarvis, business keeps moving right along."

"How is that young man?"

"Great, Pop. He's like a brother. And with him and Imani filling the gender gap, as far as siblings go, I'm not going to ask you for more."

We all laughed.

"Lawd, help!" Pop shook his head.

I had to throw in some humor somewhere to let them know that their son was still "Devin", no matter what.

With no intentions of taking that statement to heart, Mom told Pop, "He's fine, Lance...*doing real good, dear.*" She patted him on the arm.

Pop and I couldn't help it. She had tickled every funny bone in our bodies.

"I see," he said, managing to get only two words in as he slightly leaned to the side in stitches. Usually, he was cool, calm, and collected, but she had put us on another plane, which did not happen often. That was what made her statement even funnier.

No sooner had I recovered from the comedy did I turn around and wonder what could have startled the chief. What had left him speechless shaved every layer of silence. He could only say, "I can't believe it..."

I FROZE. MY OWN BEAT CAME TO A SCREECHING HALT. *I...I needed some sheet music...a chord...or a title for this mystery. Something! I heard nothing but four bass notes of mystery that lingered in my imagination and wouldn't let go. The combustion of what I saw sounded off. Dramatic. It shocked me from the intensity of disbelief. Gripping. Just as powerful as the momentum of a hurricane. Its force swept through. My scattered thoughts pounded from the heat of thumpin' strings. Without a clue, they kept ricocheting off the walls of my mind in the plains. Maybe, this was all just my imagination. I closed my eyes and reopened them but saw the same spellbinding thing. Now that I knew I was not imagining anything, the shock sent a rush down my spine. My earth quaked. Down to the core of the bone. I was left with tremors...*

...the sudden thunder of music
leaves one to wonder...

FIDDLE

Craftly designed,
fiddles are structured,
like no other kind,
a classical collection,
from ancient times.

Architecturally lovely,
by the strings of its
long and classy hair,
are played with horsehair bows,
by the fiddler's hand,
for its unique and unusual sound,
to embrace a profound legacy,
an opened book,
already acclaimed.

It's a rhythmist,
who cultivates the sound,
charting these bowed-string instruments,
deep from the root of complexities,
known for various fiddling styles,
from where it growls.
By manipulation,
they're mastered,
smoothly,
in slow-mo,
hopping and skipping,
until full moon.

…there's no comparison.

Chapter 6

NAN MOTHER

I *was locked in the mystery of the dream I was having. It seemed as though I had been in the midst of a fog for some time. However, I didn't want it to stop. A blanket of white covered only a portion of my vision. It was similar to a plasma television that displayed some of the most powerful movies but hadn't reached the top of the screen. The animations were more horizontal than vertical, but were still captivating.*

As I lay in a twilight sleep, still and stiff, I just couldn't move. My extremities tingled. So did my hands. They shook. The nerves rang throughout my body like sirens. As electrifying as it felt, my eyes seemed to race. Ranging from the global satellite of my mind, power surged all the way down the nerve endings, sending a voltage that struck like lightning bolts. It wasn't long before the quivers leveled off.

The white-powdery formation now covered the entire scope of my vision behind curtains of shuteye. Basically blindfolded, not knowing what to expect. And there were no captions either. But with great satisfaction, a burst of warmth settled within as the white formation tapered. Like a gorgeous, bright springy day, a powdered-blue background appeared. Beautiful daisies gradually populated the bottom edge of my view. They were white with yellow centered eyes. Almost as though I smelt their natural presence but, oddly, this type of flower yielded no scent. Sobeit, their presence made up for it. Wanting to touch them, I couldn't move. Nature, so beautiful but plain. As cheerful as the setting was, I felt exhilarated but not quite certain why.

Finally, a distant caption wafted through the air. Drawing my attention even more, from somewhere, I only heard voices. Or, was it only one voice? Maybe, it was just a ripple effect. Afar, it sounded very familiar. Whose voice was that? As the sound came closer, the daisies appeared to sway in one direction. They blended well. Focusing on their simple features, I immediately recognized who it was. Had I listened to Jo-Jo so much that now she appeared in my dreams? Whichever the case, I welcomed her anytime, any day. I felt like I smiled all over.

The onset scrolled up, vertically, more than before. There were flowers everywhere, crispy white, soft as doves' tails.

The sound of Jo-Jo faded as I was then captivated by another voice, "Pass this on to Devin. I would like him to have this box. He deserves it. That is a gifted young man. He is versatile and will do well. And tell him I said so." And there was not another word said.

Strangely, Jo-Jo's voice continued to vocalize without music. Then, the entire orchestra blended in on the last phrase of the melody as she articulated a compelling message, "…and, a guiding light, reveals to thee…" The bloodline of her song had a captivating pulse until it eventually flat-lined somewhere beyond the beautiful covered land. It was silent. So quiet, the daisies seemed to just listen as I did.

I twitched, again. This time, with a soft jolt.

Awakened, I whispered in the dark, "Oh, my." My eyes batted and roamed the quiet room, replaying the beautiful scene. By the time the echo of the man's voice rang out, I remembered one important matter that had not been taken care of yet. Energized, I pushed the covers aside, reached for the table lamp and turned it on. I put on my glasses. When my feet touched the floor, I slid them into my slippers.

With some sense of urgency, I walked to the foot of the bed and reached for my fuzzy, peach robe. Determined, I left the room that glowed with cherry oak Victorian furniture and charming décor. Those same daisies that had stolen my attention in the dream were the same cheery daisies that were in a vase filled with water at the center of my dresser.

There weren't too many wakeup calls like this one. It had been a while, since searching for something that had been so strongly on my mind. My belief had been to take care of important matters right away before I forgot. And since I was compelled to do so, I wouldn't be satisfied until I did.

As I headed up the hallway, I turned on the light. I went into the office that brought back so many memories. There were plaques, licenses, and diplomas hanging on the wall. Photos were artistically arranged in the most unusual collage designed by Josie, which always set-off a warm spark in my heart. She had grown attached to those photos, as had I. They were worth unspeakable words as I laid eyes on the brilliant piece of art once more. The executive desk and chair appeared peaceful in this room that held nothing but collectibles inside my very own museum full of memories. Looking for another cherished item, I opened the closet door. When I searched inside, I didn't see what I had come for. Eager, I, then, strolled into the guest bedroom. It wasn't there either. With sudden confusion, my eyebrows furrowed. There weren't too many other places it could have been. After checking a couple of other storage areas and hide-a-ways, I turned the light off and walked down the hall. At that point, I ran out of options and thought, *It'll turn up.* Surrendering the search, I walked through the doorway of the bedroom, took off my robe, and laid it in the same place as before.

The glow from the lamp that illuminated the quiet room felt welcoming. Something about its energy said it was its duty to accompany my very being, surrounding every etching of my shadow. It wasn't long before I became a captive, someone who had been mesmerized by the calming light and the effects it had cast as a soft, warm overlay. Soaked in serenity, I walked to the head of the bed. My eyes rose toward the corner of the room as I slid my feet out of my slippers. A lovely patched quilt my daughter, Judy, had given me had taken my thought away. It hung on a tall cherry-oak rack in front of a corner wall. A smile swept across my face while scanning the lovely piece of artwork until I noticed something else. As if I had seen a guiding light that had been directing the path of my eyes, I saw some cardboard exposed behind it. The blanket which had been raised on one end reminded me of a pair of eyes peeking from behind a set of drapes, but the blanket could no longer reveal what should've been concealed.

"That's strange," I said out loud, not bothering to put my slippers back on. Suspicious and without a clue, I walked to the corner wall and moved the rack to the side. A box leaned upright against the wall for support. The word FRAGILE was stamped on it several times in red. I recognized the name written on top.

"Just what I was looking for," I smiled, relieved. I thought to move it but changed my mind until the right time. "Jo-Jo, you're something else," was all I could say, tickled.

Morning came. Bright and early, a new day had been shaped with the rising of the sun. I could see and feel its radiance, waiting to burst through every crack and crevice. I peeked out the window. As the rays smiled on all things below, its beams made themselves visible. Sunlight dispersing philanthropies of goodwill could only inject its pure resources by filtering through the earth's atmosphere. It was one of those days to behold Sunday's best, a beautiful and sunshiny day that stood out above all the rest. Clearly, the day would rejuvenate everything under the sun. And for a Sunday morning, how could acts of benevolence, too, not be carried with sunlight in its purpose to the steps of the house of worship? Before long, I would reach those steps to enter, hopefully, to give and, maybe, to receive.

With that thought in mind, my day started off right as I opened the drapes. A burst of sunshine filtered through the sheers, highlighting every piece of furniture in the room. From the glory of radiance, if dust had settled anywhere, it would be conspicuous. Looking around, I could only smell the scent of lemon, wafting from the furniture polish. Some collectables glowed in sync with the rays.

When I turned around, that same Fed-Ex box was impossible to ignore. It had its own glow as I remembered taking out the contents that had greatly surprised me. The image, still fresh in my mind, was like a recently painted picture. It held deeply rooted treasures, those hard to find. I was drawn to revisit that moment, which took my attention away from doing what I had planned to do next. Anxious to get another look at what had me so puzzled, I was enticed to take that journey once more. Where it lay, I picked up the packaged tube and sat at the table. But, on second thought, as I had planned to do at first, I, instead, walked into the kitchen and made a cup of hot green tea. Mornings were incomplete without tea or some other warm drink. As an early riser, not too many days went by without it. As a routine, it was like clockwork, and, apparently, today was no different.

Back at the table, I set the cup down. In the meantime, as my tea cooled off, I opened the top of the tall triangular box and gently pulled out six posters. I stacked them into one pile across the table. For clarity and observation, I put on my glasses. My eyes lit up. All six posters were identical. Wherever the snapshot was taken, it looked so familiar.

Wasn't sure, but, what I recognized had stolen my heart. That was the one thing I was certain of. On the other hand, I was still stunned and puzzled as before, wanting to know who the sender was. Checking to make sure I hadn't missed anything, I looked inside the tube, but nothing else was there. I re-examined the small print on the label. Doing that only heightened my curiosity, rather than suspending it. Since I had no knowledge of these prints, the next thought I had was, *I wonder if—*

Immediately, I shook my head and dismissed any speculation. At that point, I was like a fiddle, waiting for a fiddler to start playing strings in my confused head, something that would sound off some familiar and relevant clues. This scenario was unlike the music previously played in my dream. Eventually, I recognized the sound, but, in this instance, I had very little to go on. There were loopholes and no answers. My thought was, *What fiddling style would the fiddler play? I'm not the rhythmist; the rhythm has already been set. I need to hear it, and I need the facts.* Without hearing a cultivated sound, I was only staring at just how complex these prints had become. For sure, whatever sound the fiddler played would be unique. I would embrace its profound legacy. Some opened-wide book had already acclaimed it, but I needed more information, which couldn't come fast enough.

The phone rang, distracting my train of thought, which burned for answers.

Removing myself from the table, I moved with a sense of urgency to answer it before whoever was calling hung up. It had already rung twice.

"Greetings," I said.

"Good morning, Nan Mother."

Immediately, I recognized the voice. "Good morning, dear. How are you on this lovely day?" I recaptured just how beautiful it was outdoors, hearing nothing but silence.

"I am fine. How are you this morning?"

Smiling at my thoughtful flower and loved one, I answered, "I'm doing just fine and am grateful, Marcella." She lit up my life, just as her children, Jay and Josie, did.

"Good. Then, we'll be by to pick you up shortly."

"Hopefully, off to the steps of freedom."

Humored, she mildly laughed and said, "Absolutely."

I beamed. Then, suddenly, the prints resurfaced and throbbed at the forefront. Before hanging up, I told her, "I'm glad you called. When time permits, there's something I would like to show you."

She would be just as shocked as I was.

…striking twist…

NOTES

Sounds of music are structured,
notes that are arranged,
displayed on the staff,
denoted by a specific character,
as a guide,
indicating duration of a tone,
by its shape,
and pitch,
by its position.

Notes are colorful,
by detail—
it intensifies,
swells,
like suspense,
or sails calmly,
whispering,
special footage,
measurements in time.

They will eventually play,
whose footprints lay,
in a musical array,
by the timing of their own music,
a pitch that is deeply rooted.

…what mosaic will notes render?

Chapter 7

CAMILLE

*As if things couldn't get any better...*I thought of home, back in Southern California on days like this. When the weather was good, I took advantage of enjoying nature and pleasant outings. This time of year, brisk, cool air had left to return next year. Now, in Atlanta, where greenery was deeply rooted for its name and richly rooted for its fame, the splendor of color had printed an interesting collage in my mind. Compressed, I revisited the outdoor scenery of this imagery. All that I had captured through the sunlight of my eyes on the land, where I sat, was etched with shrubbery and a tree or two with mature leaves. This landmark of the South had been embraced with care and nurtured by nature. The architecture seemed to smile from every angle as members and welcomed visitors entered. From very high above, a bell chimed once from the belfry.

During moments of solitude, I had to agree with Dr. Johnston. She had said it best when we met at the glory house. "This beautiful day was made to live in it," she had said. "It was made for you and for me." And that was exactly right, as I cherished those words in deep thought while sitting amongst a crowd of spirit-filled parishioners. They weren't the only ones showing some signs of life. The party

I had come with blended right in. Wide-brimmed hats were swaying, and hands were waving to heartfelt words that fell in the midst. From observation, there couldn't have been more than 250 people inside.

With all that was going on, my eyes scrubbed the sanctuary. Like some edifices, the floor slightly declined, with deep-red carpeting up the aisles. That was the one feature that immediately caught my attention while walking in. How could I not notice something that obviously displayed so much royalty? Plush and thick with padding, my shoes sank through. Felt like soft-velvety pillows. The carpet and red-cushioned pews set the color tone that contrasted perfectly with the dark wood benches that had unique carvings at each end. They appeared freshly made and had a soft sheen. Like curb appeal, the craftsman designed them using intricate detail. All rows were evenly aligned. The inside glowed with eggshell white walls and stained, soft-toned oval windows. The sun seemed to smile right through them. A few columns and an accessory of light fixtures added character. Very au courant. In comparison, it was neither a lavish place, nor a mega church, but it had just the right amount of dressings for a small congregation. The right touch gave it a peaceful appearance, a setting that exuded warmth and comfort.

As currents of energy through words of wisdom electrified the congregation, the privacy of my thoughts had been penetrated. Dr. Johnston touched me on the arm as the main attraction that stood behind the uniquely carved podium put more fuel on the fire.

"That's my daughter Judy," she let me know with an endearing smile. Dr. Johnston's charm blended well with her wardrobe. She wore a burgundy two-piece suit and sported a gorgeous hat with sparkling jewelry, but her persona radiated as the finishing touch. For the little time I'd known her, she seemed to always brighten up the atmosphere. I felt honored to know her.

Pleasantly surprised, I whispered, "Your daughter?"

"Yes," she nodded once as someone who comports oneself with dignity.

I smiled at her, then glanced back at the minister. Now that she had brought it to my attention, I saw the resemblance. Their skin tone and features were very much alike, except the daughter had dark brown shoulder-length hair. Straight, neat and softly curled under. Then, I saw a tall, distinguished, salt-and-pepper-haired gentleman stand up in her defense. He smiled at the one who had stolen the audience's attention ever since she had stood up. She showed confidence, and her articulation was crisp. She must have done this many times before as a motivational speaker. Behind her shield of honor, I detected something else. Although I didn't know her personally, I saw her as gentle but firm.

"And that's my son," Dr. Johnston, also, shared, still looking straight ahead. She wasn't about to miss anything, and I couldn't blame her. She slightly leaned in and added, "He's the one in charge."

I slightly leaned in, too, and whispered, "Pastor?"

The feathers on her hat barely moved. "Yes." She still hadn't taken her eyes off her loved one. She remained focused, in tune to the topic matter. It was almost impossible to be distracted.

Minister Judy drew so much attention to the point that she carried enough firearms in her deliverance to set off plenty of fireworks from front to back. A few toward the back stood or clapped, and some children were obviously mesmerized. On my right, Nancy, Kathy and Paula were deeply moved, enjoying this time to receive whatever they had come for. Every soul bowed on their knees. I hadn't missed a beat; I felt just as engaged as everyone else.

By the time the speaker had felt moved herself, she added more spice by saying, "I need to say something—"

"Say it!" their pastor shot back, standing not far from her.

"Hmmm," I heard Dr. Johnston say under her breath, as if she was just as inquisitive as the others were. I certainly was because I thought she had said a lot. This was getting more and more interesting by the second.

She looked into the audience and repeated, "I need to say something before I sit down. I'm enjoying this place I know…"

A lovely young lady, dressed in a choir robe, walked slowly toward her. Minister Judy briefly smiled at her as she stepped closer to someone I had not known long.

That was when the scrambling began. All at once, the director stood in front of the choir, and the musicians zipped into a musical stance.

When the two joined hands and faced the congregation, the minister added, "And I'm sure you know what I'm talking about." She had a ring in her voice.

Without prolonging the suspense, a sudden thrust of music consumed the air. An organ and piano led the way, later joined by a band of interesting instrumentalists. For a church this size, never had I seen such an array of instruments, including a harp, which was rare. It sat idle in the far corner. I guessed the song they were about to perform didn't require it. The tempo was upbeat, a rhythm that made heads bounce, hands clap, and one foot tap, or maybe even both. And I fell into each of these categories.

Nancy turned toward me. "This is special."

I smiled. "It sure is."

"I'm glad Nan Mother invited us to come."

"I am, too."

Amused, Nancy lowly chortled. "Look at him…he's having himself a good time."

My eyes followed in the same direction as hers, which focused on Dr. Johnston's son. He had the widest grin and was swaying and clapping at the same time.

I whispered back, tickled, "I see what you mean."

Drawn back to the duo, Minister Judy really did have something to say when she powerfully took to the floor and sang. It was all in her actions. She was dynamic and powerful.

Then, the young lady took it over—*Josie*. The little hostess who had served us at the home of Dr. Johnston was just as entertaining. Being captivated by someone I had not imagined could even belch notes the way she did simply amazed me. Even though she had a beautiful personality, her character belied some of her other strengths.

Soon, they both interchanged vocals as lead and backup and then together.

As far as the choir was concerned, their performance added more icing to the cake. They performed with gusto and had their own original styles. Their capacity level for creativity was open wide. As energetic as they were, it seemed as though they would never run out of gas. Then came the most stunning segment—the beat immediately halted before the finale. Changing lanes, the pace seesawed down to a slower rhythm. It reminded me of special effects, a rendition that quickly turned into slow motion. Veeeery slow—slow as the flow of molasses.

Tickled and chuckling along with the others, I leaned over, once more, and told Dr. Johnston, "I'm impressed."

This time, she looked me straight in my eyes. "And there's more," was her response, with that same endearing smile as before. And she, too, left an imprint on the imagery of my collage. All these keepsakes were compressed in my memory.

Most dispersed and left after the service, but there were still some who lingered and mingled. A preserved silence gradually covered the building to a near hush. So much action had taken place that it could only leave behind its sacred markings. Evidence of the lasting effects were still kindled by the brush of fire that had swept through. Warmth filled the place.

Before leaving, we had been introduced to and conversed with Pastor J. Kenneth Johnston and Minister Judy. When met at the path, the two were still upbeat and were lit up with southern hospitality, extending their welcome during our stay. I had nailed her personality right on the head. Just as I had summated, she was kind, and both were amiable and were the type that would attract any age group. There was no mistake that this trait had filtered down from the "queen" of their family. And somehow, I got the feeling that there was plenty more of where that had come from.

Although their time may have been limited, they were making their rounds to get acquainted with each of us. In the meantime, while moving at a snail's pace toward the exit, Dr. Johnston humorously said, "You look lovely today, Camille."

"Noooo, not I?" I humored her.

She laughed casually but kept her tone of voice down to almost a whisper.

"Thank you, Nan Mother," I finally said. "You look lovely yourself."

"Thanks the same, dear." In confidence, she leaned inward and said absorbingly, "Never change. I like your spirit. All fashions are not in style; neither are they appealing."

I didn't quite get it, so, I asked for clarity, "I'm sorry, but I didn't get the connection, Nan Mother." I smiled at the stunning antique. Very interested in hearing her response, I locked arms with hers as we coasted along, lagging behind the others like best friends.

She looked me in the eyes. "What part?"

"When you said, 'All fashions are not in style; neither are they appealing.' "

A soft smile colored her face. "The person that you are is very fashionable, meaning likeable, and it is stylish and will appeal to most people."

"Oooh," I said.

"You have them both."

"That's nice to hear. Thank you."

She nodded, "You're welcome."

When I looked ahead, the others had walked on out, beyond the white, double French doors, but her son was waiting for us patiently.

Dr. Johnston had made a statement, one she apparently did not want me to forget. How could I? She reminded me of someone back home when it came to defining their choice of words.

She stopped. "Oh! And one other thing while it's on my mind."

"Sure, Nan Mother. What is it?"

"That fella you know…Devin Fairchild."

"Yes," I looked at her again with curiosity.

"I knew I had heard that name before. Is there some way of getting in contact with him?"

"Yes, there is. Is there something I can do?"

"Dear, there is something you can do for me. I really need to speak with him if that can be arranged."

"Sure. I know someone who can, definitely, make it happen."

"Ooh, thank you," she said, relieved. "I made a promise that I must keep."

"I'll make that call today."

She nodded with gratitude and then asked another question before reaching the exit. "Did you say you live in California?"

"I did," I answered, stating the city I lived in, too.

She smiled. "Hopefully, I'll get a chance to see you during my visit in the coming months."

"That would be great." I stopped for a moment and removed my shoulder bag. "Let me give you a card with my contact information." When I opened it, something stood out. I had only one thought. As I pulled it out, I said as I handed it to her, "Something for you." How could I not? It felt so right.

She looked puzzled and took what was inside out and read it quietly. When she finished, she gave her approval, "For you, dear, I'll be there. Our family had already planned a trip to California. That's perfect timing. I would love to."

I whispered, "You're the only one who knows."

"The only one?" she appeared shocked.

"Yes."

"Oh, my," was all she said.

Not only was she surprised—the topic about Devin had surprised me, also. As interesting as the day had been, I had heard many musical notes that I could relate to and understand. But...this unexpectedly new revelation had stunned me. Perplexed, I was unable to make any musical sense out of it. I was at a loss for its beat and the words. The sound from this topic was already intensified, and the suspense was swelling. The thoughts that queried could not be shaken. *What note was that? The duration of the tone had a dramatic sound. What could be the connection? Would the unknown be just as mysterious? And would the notes of the missing links be colorful?* They would have to be coded with special footage, measurements in time of a topic matter that was so important to her. I could only wonder about the whispering suspense as it eventually and calmly sailed. *Every missing note will eventually be played*, I told myself, *all in a musical array by duration and pitch.* I had a feeling that the outcome would be deeply rooted. But "what?" was the BIG question.

…this beat of stunning notes
drew attention…

DRUM ROLL

Drums are famous for their purpose,
the captain of rhythm,
nucleus of music,
a percussion instrument,
with a strong heartbeat.

On its platform,
drum rolls spin,
striking the target seat,
of its skin,
before it leaps,
to surf currents of music,
thriving in the heat.

Drum rolls are like an introduction,
grand and stylishly captivating,
as a suction,
skipping,
repeating,
its mysterious spin,
into a rhythmic mound,
growing its grin,
shaped from its animated sound,
webbed by the mystery it holds,
infused with suspense,
to unfold.

…drum rolls are famous for revealing its teeth.

Chapter 8

DEVIN

I had stared at a repeat that kept skipping right in front of my eyes. Drum rolls skillfully spinning, swirling thoughts of confusion. Too much like a grand introduction, leading up to some suspense, growing in its grin the entire time. *How mysterious is that?* When I thought how captivating it was, all I could think of was, *What does this have to do with someone I have never met or seen before?*

It has been said that we all have a twin, but I had to shake that one off. How could someone look so much like someone from the past? Since so much had gone on yesterday at the family reunion, the thought vanished, but only temporarily—I had been entertained well. Furthermore, the person in question had come and gone. Undoubtedly, the time would come to inquire.

The day had been refreshing. Sundays were usually good, especially a day that wouldn't be complete without special visitation rights. Those rights summoned me to pay my respects to the Man Upstairs. Not only had I welcomed the invitation, but relatives had come to begin a new day filled with sunshine. It was as if the radiance had supplied us with plenty of its supplements because the beauty of it all had filled the place with gratitude. *That was nice*, I thought. The morning service had made my day.

As I parked in front of the hotel across from Stonecrest Mall, I noticed a car as it passed by not far away. The driver resembled someone from back home, but, being in Atlanta, I knew that wasn't possible.

On my way toward the hotel entrance, my cell phone rang as the corridor opened. I recognized the number and flipped it up.

"Is this who I think it is?" I joked. I knew exactly who had rung. It was a good change of pace to get a call from a friend back in sunny California.

"Yes, it is," Jarvis replied with a chuckle.

At the right place at the right time, I headed toward a nearby table in the dining area. There were no other customers in the empty room. Only the game televised on the flat screen television filled the air. I had all the privacy that I needed.

"Man, I had to sit down. This call probably warrants a drink."

"Hopefully, Kool-Aid," he reminded me because that was a conversation piece we had entertained many times before. Usually, the joke was on him.

"I have to pass on that one. That's not good enough," I told him, as an attendant approached my table after I had gotten his attention. I pointed at what I wanted on the menu.

"Oooh. Well, what is?"

"Cranberry juice will suffice." When I answered Jarvis's question, the attendant thought I was talking to him. The timing could not have been better.

"Good answer. You had me wondering for a second. You don't need anything that will make you curl up like shrimps."

I chuckled. "Yeah. All right."

He refreshed my memory. Still fresh on my mind, I wondered where Jarvis could have come up with a script like that—curl up like shrimps. Never had I heard that one before.

Changing the subject, he asked, "How's it going in the South?"

"I'm enjoying every bit of it. The weather is nice, and I'm glad to see family."

"I know that's right, bruh. How are they doing?"

"Fine. Pop asked about you."

"Tell him I hope to be heading up his way real soon."

"Will do."

"The reason why I called," his tone of voice changed, "is quite interesting." Knowing him, it either had to be something related to business, or something that was completely baffling, that demanded immediate attention.

Since I wasn't sure, I asked, "Does this conversation require something stronger than cranberry juice?" I didn't know what to expect when he made questionable statements like that. I had dangled from one cliffhanger too many not to know that somehow I may need some help making an impromptu decision, unless it was strictly related to him.

He chuckled before responding, "I doubt it, but it's enough to make you wonder. Long and hard."

The attendant returned and set the glass of cranberry juice in front of me.

"Thank you," I whispered.

He nodded.

Without losing my train of thought, I replied, "I was only kidding, but what would make me think long and hard, Jarvis? Is it that serious?"

"Maybe not. You may already be aware or know something about the message that I have been asked to pass on to you."

I sipped some cranberry juice before asking the next question. "And what would that be? I'm all ears." I set the glass back down on the table.

"Camille—"

Before he could get out good what he wanted me to know, I said, mystified, "Camille?"

"Yes, Camille. She's the messenger, just a step away from you."

Almost at a whisper, the next question zipped from my mouth, "Camille is in Atlanta?"

"She is and has been there for a couple of days."

"You had mentioned some weeks ago that she had planned a trip to Atlanta, but, for some reason, I got the dates mixed up."

"She met some friends there. Girlfriends' weekend escape or something to that effect. But anyway," he said, getting back to why he had called, "someone she met in Atlanta wants to speak with you, if it can be arranged."

Baffled, I muttered, "Wants to speak with me..." My words trailed; I felt like I could've been many miles away in thought.

"Whatever the reason, according to Camille, it's important that she speak with you."

My next question was, "Who is she?"

"Hold on," Jarvis said. In the background, I heard him rumbling through papers. "I have it written down right here. Her name is...Dr. Johnston."

Since that didn't ring a bell, I, then, asked, "What is her first name?"

"Camille called her 'Nan Mother.'"

I emphasized, "Dr. Nan Mother Johnston?"

"That's what she said. Sounds like a nickname to me, bruh."

"Sounds like it to me, too." I thought hard to remember if I knew of anyone with that last name. "Dr. Johnston," I said repeatedly.

"Any clues?" I heard Jarvis say in-between the blanks. Still at a loss, I had no idea who that person could be.

I slowly shook my head. "None I can think of. You were right."

"About what?"

"That I would think long and hard."

"Well, I'm about to put the icing on the cake. There's one other thing."

I became completely silent. The thoughts that had been ticking inside my head came to a screeching halt.

He added, "Camille said that her exact words were, 'I made a promise I must keep.'"

I didn't say a word. Because I was still dressed in a suit, I loosened my necktie. This piece of information was too strange.

Further, he said, "Camille was even surprised about it, but she seems to have grown fond of this lady."

"Do you have some idea of her age?" I couldn't resist asking as I reached inside my jacket for a pen and miniature notepad to write down her name. If at all, maybe that would help. I felt a little relieved in knowing that Camille had taken a liking to her.

"She didn't say. With a name like that, she has to be an older woman."

"You may be right, but I'm not so sure about that."

"From the way Camille was talking, it's worth looking into. You never know about things like this. Maybe, her name will register later."

"Is there more that you need to tell me?"

"I wish I could say yes. That's all the information I've been given."

"Maaan," I said as if hesitant about moving forward with this, "your call is enough to make anybody curl. That's pretty strong to digest. This news is more than what I expected, and I have very little information to go on."

"I was hoping you knew this lady. Since you don't, would you like for me to call Camille and see what more I can find out? That's not a problem." Jarvis seemed just as interested in knowing who would pass along such a skeletal message to someone they had never met.

"Thanks. That won't be necessary. I'll give her a call today. This is a drum roll that has left too much for the imagination." I could only ask myself, *Could she be an admirer? But that doesn't make sense if she made a promise she must keep.*

"I hear where you're coming from. There are too many loose ends, right?"

I picked the glass up off the table and momentarily looked at the ruby-red substance. "Absolutely." Tilting the glass up, I drank another sip, then put it back down before the countdown to consume the rest.

Finally, I said, "What is her contact number?"

After Jarvis gave it to me, he switched lanes and wanted to hear more about my visit to Atlanta. Picking up where we left off, he said, "Your family picked a good time to have a reunion."

Dropping the conversation that had me so baffled was a good change of pace. For the time being, I needed to concentrate on something other than another mystery. I responded, "It's perfect. Not too hot and not cold either." Although we had changed the subject, it took a minute to wipe that topic off the slate of my mind.

"Never thought about having one during the month of May. I have only known of reunions taking place during primetime."

Puzzled, I asked, "What do you mean by 'primetime'?" That was Jarvis. Every now and then, he had me guessing at some of his unusual phrases, but that was just his way of thinking and his way of expressing himself.

After realizing that he needed to be more specific, he answered, "Primetime…right in the heart of the hot, hot weather, which is just around the corner."

"Oh," my head bounced, "that's what you meant. I get what you're saying. Sometimes, the heat can be overbearing. I'm glad they decided to have it sooner, and so was everyone else, from what I hear."

"Speaking of the others…I know you were glad to see relatives you hadn't seen in a while."

"Yes, I was. Some were there this time that I hadn't seen since my high school days, but there was this one guy I had never seen. Spooked me, man."

Silence fell.

Momentarily, I reflected on how Pops had reacted. He couldn't believe his eyes. Neither could I.

All of a sudden, Jarvis laughed out, then said hilariously, "From the way that sounded, all I could see was you running, Devin. That last statement made me rise up in my chair."

"I'm sure it did." Drafted by his sense of humor, it didn't take long before I joined in his moment of laughter.

"I'm anxious to know what that's all about."

"You want to know? Brutha…so do I!"

"Hold that thought," he said with urgency. "I'm going to put you on hold for a moment."

"Sure." Immediately, I drifted.

Revisiting this segment had me just as bewildered as the topic about Dr. Nan Mother Johnston. Seemed like we were bouncing from one puzzling ordeal to the next. *Two drum rolls?* From the sound of it, the rolls would definitely leap to thrive in the heat of some music unknown to me. *Could I possibly know this song?* was another thought. *Maybe, an oldie but goodie.* I don't know, but its heartbeat was strong, webbed by some mystery, infused with suspense. I had mixed feelings, and, if it weren't for Camille entertaining the issue, I probably would've dismissed it. At this point, what had felt like a grand entrance was too much and too early to be figured out. Confused, I could only wait for the music of complexity to unfold.

Snapped out of wonderland, Jarvis returned and commented as if there had never been any break in conversation, "You have had some jaw-dropping experiences in your lifetime, but I have to admit that those experiences, so far, have been worth it. They're keepsakes to cherish for life. And there are no replacements."

"Yeah, you're right," I told him, smiling, as I thought back on some of those special moments. "Unbelievable."

"Umph…I'm curious now. I wonder who that guy is."

The phone went dead.

...strange beat...

PACE

Pace has character,
in its rate of movement,
an interesting bloodline,
by style as its trait,
but,
without timing,
it's colorblind.

Like profiles,
some paces are unique,
with visages,
striking eyes,
shadowed,
by what lies within,
searching,
deep in its lens,
for the speed of its music,
hints,
to be revealed,
traces of evidence.

It's eye-catching,
when its eyebrows twitch,
a speed regulator,
fluctuating the switch,
to bleed its natural beauty.

...climates of speed ages with time.

Chapter 9

NAN MOTHER

"Ooooo, child! You know you have it in you. Don't you?"

Josie let out an unusually shy giggle. She put her head on my shoulder. "Nan Mother, I learned from you."

I slowed the pace down, playing the piano that seldom exercised its lungs. Sitting next to Josie on the cushioned bench, I looked toward her as she lifted her head, "Me?"

We both found humor in my quick response.

The upright still had it, ringing out notes, stretching from high to low on the scale. It had had many days of rest, sitting idle in the family room, but, today, it had, once again, made the most beautiful sound. I had not majored in music, but, during my younger days, I had learned a little and picked up more over the years. Often thought about the field of musicology but went another direction. And singing had not been my greatest strength, but I knew good singing when I heard it. That was why I couldn't imagine what on earth Josie was talking about.

"What about singing could you have possibly learned from me, dear? Not Nan Mother?"

"Yeeees," she softly answered me. Then, she continued her role, singing, while, swaying her head. Her way of keeping beat. We were, as they say, "walking and chewing gum at the same time." Spurts of conversation were not an interruption. It blended right in.

I proceeded, "You must have me mixed up with someone else." I chuckled at the thought, glancing once more at the teen, now a young lady, that I had had many conversations with.

Grinning, she kept motioning her head to the rhythm, and so did I.

I kept right on playing, intrigued by the direction in which this conversation had turned.

Almost like the game of musical chairs, she decided to reply during the perfect break when she could speak in-between her lines. At once, she stole her moment to rhythmically say, "You don't remember, Nan Mother?" Her voice went up a notch. I could tell she enjoyed seesawing with the pace. This was a style she had cleverly mastered.

"Hmmmm," I thought twice before speaking again. It sounded like I was humming to the music rather than trying to recall something. As important as this was, I couldn't see how it could have slipped my mind. *Certainly, I would have remembered that.*

"Hmmmm," she followed with her index finger pressed against her temple. Simply an indication as to when she felt ready to tell me. That was all part of her game.

Only because of curiosity, I repeated the same word as before. Brief and short. Since some of the letters of my reply were dropped, I no longer sounded like a part of this exercise. I had already lost this game but, I felt ready to try it again.

Josie repeated herself, as well. She looked as though she would burst, but she held out as long as she could.

Tickled myself, I came close to stopping the music.

Surprised that she wanted to continue after running out of breath rather than taking a break, she motioned with her hand to keep playing before I stopped. When she quickly composed herself and felt ready, she started again.

"Weeeell," I joined in, waiting for a reply.

She shook her head, trying to focus. She snickered then playfully said in a context that I couldn't recall ever hearing her say before, "Movin'…movin'…ri-ight along."

Startled, I stared at her, then inquired, "Josie, what kind of word is that? Movin'?" I got straight to the point. Straight talk.

She snickered again. "It's just slang, an invented word, Nan Mother. That's all." Then, she picked up where she had left off.

"Ummm hmmm," trailed from my mouth steadily.

"Do you remem-m-m-m-m-ber when—"

With more emphasis, I cut in, in a hurry, "Ummmmmm hmmmmmmm."

This time, more legs had crawled and connected to additional consonants. Even the beat revved up a little. My intentions were to boost her into telling me exactly what was on her mind.

"You can stop…the music."

I stopped playing.

"You told me to remember Jo-Jo—that she would be part of the key to my gifted abilities."

"Ooooh."

"You did say-ay-ay that. Do-o-o you re-mem-m-m-ber?"

I was impressed that she sang those words as creatively as she had. I smiled and leaned toward her and followed her lead the best I could. "Yeeees," I verified. "I-I re-mem-m-ber." I chuckled, failing some octaves. Besides that, I missed some of the vocal curves to make it sound more magical, but

I could have cared the least. It was all for fun as I enjoyed my Josie.

She lightly clapped, showing her approval.

Dropping my part of the act, I clapped with her and told her, "Nan Mother hasn't forgotten."

"That's all folks!"

"Bugs Bunny! Now, that…I haven't forgotten." So tickled, my equilibrium felt off balance. Unexpectedly, she completely stung my knapsack, reminding me of a character so old but yet so young in a child's mind. That warranted me to reflect on when the "original cartoons" had been popular. Those animated icons had basically taken over the networks; the marathons ran for hours. Nonstop. Practically half the day. Probably would have never given Bugs Bunny another thought if Josie hadn't mentioned it. On second thought, that was impossible since I had taken photos with this character in the past.

Here we were, both laughing at her spontaneous humor. Only Josie, De, and her brother knew how to keep me going. They were a patchwork of joy. All three.

I got up from the bench and went to sit in the recliner, still tickled and trying to shake it off the tip of my brain. "Lawd, Lawd, Lawd." I blew out a sudden rush of air as I sat to relax.

"Nan Mother," she said as she got up, "would you like a cold drink?"

"Dear, that sounds good."

Josie whisked into the kitchen.

"Now…you hold that thought," I told her.

"I will," her voice trailed from another room.

When she returned, she brought me a tall glass of sweet tea along with a turkey sandwich.

With gratitude, as I reached for the tray from inside the recliner's pouch, I said, "Oooh, dear…thank you." I hadn't realized how hungry I was, so I was elated when she brought a snack, too.

"You're welcome."

"You knew just what I needed. Are you going to get something to eat yourself?"

She smiled and, as she headed back to the kitchen, said, "Yes. I'll join you."

On her return, she sat on the sofa. "I'm surprised, Nan Mother, that you haven't turned the stereo on to listen to Jo-Jo."

"Honey, I've heard enough singing to last me the rest of the day. And everything that I have already heard has been a delight. That includes you."

Josie blushed and sipped her drink. As she placed her glass on a cup mat, she asked, "How did I do?"

My eyes slightly stretched. "You were outstanding, dear." It clearly indicated that she deserved high marks.

"That's what Mom said."

"Marcella's right. You were," I reassured her before I took another swallow of the cold, satiating drink.

She added, "Jay commented, too."

I put my glass down. "What did he say?"

"The same thing."

As I imagined seeing his face and reaction, I slightly grinned. "You know, if Jay thought so, that's saying a lot. He speaks exactly what's on his mind."

Josie softly chuckled. "He sure does." She nodded her head, knowing that I had made a valid point. It couldn't be denied. Her brother had always been honest with her about anything she did. Quite frankly, he was honest about most things. That was probably what had helped her work harder.

One could only wonder why she would ask that question. I had to find out what was on her mind after we had indulged into our sandwiches. "Why did you ask?"

Inspiration glowed in her eyes. "Someday, I want to sing like Jo-Jo. I've always remembered when you told me that she would be a part of the key to my gifted abilities."

"Ooh," I nodded, slowly. "I see."

My response seemed to have humored her a little. She picked up her sandwich and bit into it, and I joined her. Afterwards, I took advantage of an open window.

After swallowing, I spoke with concern. "Dear, you have great capabilities and a style all of your own. I want you to excel and be great, but you can only be the person that you are. And that is Josie Rose. And you are a rose. Whenever you sing, you emit a fragrance that people just love to smell."

She stopped what she was doing. "I've never heard that before, Nan Mother," she said comically. "Fragrance? Smell?" Confusion seemed to have run all through her expression.

Tickled, I explained, "You emit the fragrance of your gifted abilities, which gives so much joy to those who are listening. They inhale every note of music that you sing. We knew you would be a rose."

"That's why you named me that?" She smiled because of the exegesis of a new discovery. Her expression revealed that she had just heard an astonishing disclosure. She knew that I had named her but had never known why. However, I did name her, also, for another reason. Before I was done, she would, most likely, figure that out.

"Yes, at your parents' request. But remember, Jo-Jo is Jo-Jo…Josie Rose is Josie Rose. I told you to remember Jo-Jo as an inspiration. Not to duplicate her. Hopefully, her gift has inspired you."

"She has," she nodded and assured me. "I'm connected; I can relate to her."

"Come again, Josie Rose?"

"I'm connected, and I can relate to her."

Since she piqued my curiosity, I wanted to hear more about the stimulation of where that had come from, so I asked her, "How so?"

We both took a minute to bite into our sandwiches before she continued. There was no hurry. I had plenty of time to listen to what she had to say. What affected her life had always been important to me. She knew Nan Mother didn't mind and always cared.

She cleared her throat. "I feel as though I connect with the rhythm of her music. When it speaks within, deep down, she answers. When it whispers, she listens for the flow."

Once again, I couldn't help but say, "Come again, Josie Rose?" She had my undivided attention.

The second time around, she repeated herself slower than before, but I couldn't quite put my finger on the analogy. "The flow of what, dear?" *Did she mean the lyrics or the music?*

"She listens for the flow of sweet honey. Sweet honey is the lyrics of her rhythm that flows."

That phrase hung like a banner. "Hmmm."

She further explained, "It has a way of dancing around in a person's heart until it passes through as a rush, or it will come through slowly, smoothly, and calmly. Either way, it electrifies her output and dances right on out of her vocal canal."

All I could do, for the moment, was watch it precipitate inside my cerebellum. Then, I said, "Lawd…Lawd…Lawd, where did that come from?" Snowflakes of understanding fell.

My reaction had surprised her. Humbly, she grinned from the spontaneous remark as she reached for her glass again.

"Is there anything else that you would like to add?" I asked.

After a couple of swallows, she put her glass down. "That's all, Nan Mother. I'm done."

"You've said more than what's on your plate, dear. I'm glad you've shared that with me."

"That's how I see it."

"Jo-Jo sounds like the gold that sweet honey, musically, is made of. Doesn't she?"

Agreeing, she nodded. "She does. Since kindergarten, listening to her has always been inspiring."

"I recall. You used to sing along with her every time you heard her voice. And that brings me back to my point. As long as you remember her as a source of inspiration, she will be a fragment of your success. Because you know where your talent comes from." My voice had shot up a notch with emphasis. I changed the pace, purposely adding a little humor, which made her chuckle, but she understood where all blessings came from. "One last thing," I continued.

She looked toward me and listened. At the same time, she picked up what was left of her sandwich and bit into it once more.

"It doesn't matter how great of a singer you are. The sweet honey that you can relate to comes from the heart. It's in a humbling place because you do not put yourself above others. Treat it with care. No one can take that away from you."

"I will hold on to that, Nan Mother," she glistened. "Always."

Two seconds didn't pass before the phone rang.

Josie got up. "I'll get it."

"Nan Mother appreciates that."

I had enjoyed the pace of this entire conversation. Unique by trait. So colorful. If it hadn't been for perfect, rhythmic timing, the character of its pace would've been colorblind, which meant it would have had no precision of style. The profile of the conversation was interesting...the right speed of music. Certainly wouldn't have been surprised if its eyebrows had twitched, again, at a later date, to some other topic raised, bleeding its natural beauty.

That thought washed away when Josie quickly rushed toward me. From her sudden reaction, I knew that my next bite into my sandwich would have to wait. Pressing the phone tightly in the palm of her hand for confidentiality, she whispered excitedly, "Is this who I think it is?"

Confusion must've been written entirely across my face as I said, "Well…I don't know. Who is it?"

"You know, Nan Mother! That famous guy! Devin Fairchild!"

The doorbell rang.

We both flinched from the sudden interruption.

...rewind...

CHANT

Interesting by style,
presentations,
chants are words uttered,
recited,
a manner of singing,
or,
speaking in musical monotones.

A chant is a repetitive melody,
profound moments,
of several words sung to one tone—
oftentimes,
a twist,
before touchdown,
for the final bliss.

They are formulations,
melodramas,
percolating,
emitting colorful faces,
carved and cultivated,
from mirrored tunes,
sketched and autographed,
to savor.

…spoken arts are spectacular-musical paintings.

Chapter 10

CAMILLE

I closed my planner. "That covers it, lady friends," I said, after filling them in on the details. Jarvis's birthday gathering was only months away. The weekend had been perfect, the opportune time to finalize loose ends for planning.

Paula smiled. "This is exciting, Camille. It won't be long."

"In a blink," I responded. "I will keep you all posted."

Kathy chimed in, "I'm looking forward to it. It's about time for another after-five event."

"I agree," Nancy chirped. "I mentioned it to Larry, and he was elated and impressed at the same time."

Curiously, I stated, "I wonder, what ran across his mind?"

Nancy shook her head with a gleam in her eyes. "He chortled and said, 'It's going to be an interesting day. I love it.' "

All eyes were glued on her. Larry's comments had been placed under observation. She had our undivided attention. I could only smile.

Entertaining that thought, Paula asked Nancy, "And that's it?" Evidently, she was baffled.

"Yes, that's all he said. A little strange, I thought."

Paula appeared bemused. "That is an interesting statement."

"I thought so, too," was my response. "Maybe, Larry has something in store for you, Nancy."

She drifted off in thought for a moment, then said, "It's not my birthday. If he does have something in mind, he's being very quiet about it."

Kathy opened the palms of her hands. "Hmmm," was all she said, thinking. She had run out of options. There was neither anything else to say, nor was there anything else she could have said that would have validated just what Larry meant. Her guess would have been just another speculation.

"Maybe, it's nothing at all," I told them. "If it was, only he could answer that question for us."

Paula humored us, "Honey, watch out!"

We laughed.

Kathy didn't quite seem to buy it either. "I have to agree with Paula. I don't know about that one. His comments are tricky."

Nancy stated, "I zeroed in on the phrase when he said, 'It's going to be an interesting day.' What could be so interesting about a birthday celebration? We've been to others before." The more she thought about it, the more her curiosity heightened.

"Exactly," Paula replied.

Although I felt the same way, I remained neutral. "Maybe and maybe not. We'll see in the coming months."

That topic came to a halt when we noticed that Paula's eyes had frozen in midair. "Isn't that Devin Fairchild?" A smile gently crept across her face.

I turned my head. "It sure is." I smiled, then stood up. "Excuse me. There's something I must take care of." I went to catch-up with him before he got away.

Alone, he casually walked the aisle. Sunrays through the skylight clearly revealed his identity. His signature made him stand out. He was always clean-cut and neatly dressed. His profile was hard to miss, especially to those who knew him well. Since he was taller than most, I could follow him easily.

Trying to get around the crowd with more speed than normal created a sudden adrenaline rush. Just at the right time, as I got closer, the coast became clear. When he spotted me, he smiled brightly and met me at the path.

Glad to see another familiar face, I smiled, too.

He shook his head and, sounding upbeat, said, "Umph, umph, umph, did you follow me to Atlanta?"

Everyone who knew him well knew he had a comical side. I was very familiar with it. He had a colorful sense of humor that most liked about him.

His comment had hit a funny bone, and, before I realized it, I was swept away by laughter.

Devin chuckled. "It's alright, Miss C. Would you like a handkerchief?" He reached in his pocket and pulled one out.

"No, thanks. I'll be fine." My eyes were watery but soon dried-up.

Seeing that we were in the path of oncoming shoppers, we walked to a more suitable area for conversation.

"Although I didn't follow you to Atlanta, it's good to see you, Devin."

He put the handkerchief back in his pocket. "Likewise. It's especially a good surprise to run into someone from up my way."

In agreement, I told him, "This is a surprise, especially seeing you. Usually, when you're out of town, you're on an expedition."

"Usually," he nodded his head, "but not this time."

"I know. Otherwise, your business partner would be here, too."

"As a matter-of-fact, I just spoke with Jarvis not long ago."

"Did you?" my voice elevated when I learned that he had received a call from him so quickly, knowing that I had spoken to him myself not long ago.

Devin slightly bowed his head, "Yes, I did, Your Highness. He told me that you were here in Atlanta."

We both took a moment and chuckled at his humorous comment.

After a few seconds, he said, "First of all, let me start over again. How have you been?"

"Great. And yourself?"

"Can't complain. Hope you're enjoying your trip?"

"I really am. Thank you. I'm having a good time here in the South. Some friends and I decided to get together for the weekend. We couldn't have picked a better time. The weather complimented it all."

"Absolutely. I have to say the same. This is some great weather. I do not believe we could've picked a more suitable time to have a family reunion."

"Fortunately, it's not steaming hot."

"And that's how I like it."

"So do I, Devin. And, by the way," I decided to take this opportunity to get to a very important matter, "while I'm thinking about it, did Jarvis give you my message?"

The expression on his face said it all. "Whew," he blew out as if extremely confused. "Yes, he did." His eyebrows were knitted. I could never recall ever seeing him that puzzled. Just the same, I didn't have a clue. Within a short period of time, I had met this wonderful lady who I admired and who had welcomed my friends and me into her home like family. As if everything had been planned, as destiny would have it, now Devin had become the center attraction of this mystery.

From his reaction, I had to ask myself again, *Who is Nan Mother, and what is the connection?* Those words were brightly blinking inside my head as I quietly chanted them. They were musical monotones, a profound moment. Reminded me of a melodrama. Devin and Dr. Johnston's actions were slowly smoking before my eyes. But what was the plot? I, then, said, "I see confusion knocking on your door." Since I knew no more than he did, I was still stuck on one note, bewildered. It had a strong pulse, like the conversation I'd had earlier with Dr. Johnston. The chant percolated, again, in my thoughts as others trailed in line. *What color face will eventually emit from between the two?* Hopefully, the ending would be colorful, a final bliss. So far, the style had been interesting. There were not enough tunes to go on. All I could do, for the moment, was savor the sketched, mirrored tone of the dramatic chant.

"Camille, you have no idea." Then, he asked, "Who is this lady?"

Although puzzled, an image of Dr. Johnston and our earlier conversation resurfaced. As the messenger, I shared with him, slightly smiling with delight, "My stay in Atlanta has been great, as well as interesting. Through one of my girlfriends, I was introduced to Dr. Johnston. She is Nancy's neighbor. Very nice lady. Getting right to what I need to tell you, I think, would only confuse you more."

"What would that be?"

"Her exact words were, 'I made a promise I must keep.' "

"Umph," Devin pondered on that declaration. Even though Jarvis had passed along the same message, he felt as though he had heard it for the very first time. "And she said…nothing else?"

I slightly shrugged my shoulders. "Nothing else, other than that she really needs to speak with you. She wanted to know if I could arrange that." I wished I could've told him more, but, before this conversation ended, I told him, "Friend to friend...you should give her a call. Sounds very important. If it helps, I felt very comfortable with her, as everyone else did. If there had been any signs of caution, I would not have bothered you or Jarvis, nor, would I have wasted my time."

"I hear what you're saying, Camille," he smiled down at me with appreciation. "I did give her a call this afternoon."

"Good." Then, I thought, *How is it that he still doesn't know who she is?* Apparently, my expression had said it all.

Before asking him anything further, he explained, "She had visitors, so I told her I would call back this evening."

Now, I understood. "That makes sense."

He noticed, as I did, that he was getting plenty of stares. He put his dark shades on and continued, "I'm glad we had this conversation because I was reluctant when Jarvis relayed the message."

"I thought you would feel that way, and I understand why. If reversed, I would most likely be hesitant, too."

"You are a special lady, Camille, and Jarvis knows that. He has told me so, and I agree with him. If it weren't for that and your intuitiveness, I would not have given it a second thought."

"Thank you for the compliment."

"Compliment deserved." Then, something else hit him. "There is one other thing I would like to ask."

"Sure."

"How does she know me?"

"Oh, I almost forgot. While we were at her house, we were listening to music. I had said that I knew of someone who would really appreciate the songster's voice we were listening to. She became curious and wanted to know whom.

So, I told her, 'Devin Fairchild.' From my reply, she appeared to be a million miles away. Then, she said, 'That name is very familiar.' "

Trying to make sense out of that, he proceeded, "She's probably trying to connect me with my career. It's not like no one knows. You think maybe that's it, as far as that is concerned?"

Doubtfully, I answered, shaking my head, "I...don't think so. She strongly emphasized the word 'very.' "

"Really?" Devin slightly shook his head as if all that I had said just wasn't quite sinking in. Or maybe it had. Either way, I figured he'd find out soon enough.

"Honestly, I don't think you'll regret it. And, before it's all over, you'll be calling her Nan Mother, too. Take my word for it."

He gleamed with a smile. "I've heard all I needed to hear."

...the chants of suspense are mesmerizing...

PAUSE

Chapter 11

DEVIN

Since it was a holiday weekend, I wasn't surprised that merchants were jumpstarting the holiday by allowing shoppers to take advantage of their sales. With this kind of weather, how could they lose? Although unpredictable, sunshine was the perfect package deal that tended to get people out, even if they just window shopped. And Stonecrest Mall drew them in. It was the hot spot that lured me, too, and where I, ironically, ran into Camille.

Being overcome by a fraction of what I knew, what more I wanted to know about Dr. Johnston, and a runaway imagination had me going. So far, I'd heard voices without faces, a bass, and drum rolls. And they were voices I didn't even recognize. Still blindfolded by the suspense, the "promise" couldn't come soon enough. The searchlight oscillated through my consciousness for any clues I could grasp. The only thing I knew, for sure, was her name. The combination of all three, eventually, set me on another course—I had an agenda. During this trip, there were people to see and places to go. So, I decided to put all the intricate music—imagined—on pause. For the time being, I needed to clear my head and give it a rest.

My excursion had set sail down Peachtree Street. By five o'clock, Imani and I were at a restaurant, where stakes were driven as one of the many popular places for dining. People were out in full force. It was packed but comfortable. Pleasantly engaged and impressed by their cultural hospitality, I mentally had formed roots as a place notated to revisit.

Being in a different environment took me on mental journeys. During times like these, I thought about family, friends, and years gone by. I even dreamed a little—without smooth tea—or rewound special Kodak moments. And that was just what happened. I guess I had needed a good laugh because my brain tripped the wires of my imagination elsewhere, temporarily, while waiting for Imani to return. While going back down memory lane, I thought about the gorilla incident. How many times had I retold that story of the West? Hard to believe and imagine but true. Laughing within and on the verge of busting up, I could only shake my head, just as Imani returned to our table.

She sat down. "It's obvious that something is on your mind." She overlapped her arms, resting them in front of her, full of wonder. Her eyes sparkled brightly.

Entertaining the thought, I told her, "It definitely is. Sis, I had rewound the time back on one particular moment that could *never*...and I mean...*never* be erased from inside my head. And you don't have to think long and hard about that one."

Tickled, she asked for confirmation, "It has to be about that gorilla that escaped from its cage at the state fair in Phoenix and ran everybody away as they screamed loudly and panicked." She felt almost sure she had it right.

"You nailed it on the head."

"And you didn't even have to ask," Imani joked. "I wish I could have seen our grandmother running, leaving you behind."

She laughed just as I had.

I shook my head, "Who would have ever thought that? When you're scared, you do things you never thought you could do." Trying to imagine her running with that kind of speed made my eyes water even more. I pulled out my handkerchief.

"She proved it, didn't she?"

"That's an understatement!" I wiped my eyes, then inserted the handkerchief back into my pocket.

Imani wiped hers, too, with a tissue she had retrieved from her purse.

"Come to think of it," I said, as something occurred to me, "that was the last time I can recall her ever going back. She stuck with Jesus; she'd seen all she needed to see." And I let it rest.

Agreeing, Imani admitted like a witness would, "I know that's right." She put the tissue back in her purse. "Although, my initial thought had reverted to that snake. Remember that one?"

"The snake…" I mumbled, trying to let that statement filter through.

"Yes, the snake in the church," she grinned uncontrollably.

I saw where this was going. Two comical incidents, back-to-back, would only fill our eyes with water again. I had already laughed to the point that the back of my ears throbbed. Imani sparked me to eject right back in time when I suddenly remembered. "Oh, that's right. Fright night," I chortled, absorbed by another masterpiece, regarding a snapshot that could hang on anyone's wall to be looked at anytime. Without a doubt, they would be instantly cured. Some exposures were unbelievable and just as potent as laughing gas. They were hard to come by, just like the gorilla story. Reaching back in my pocket, I pulled out my handkerchief again. Imani became a blur in front of me. The word "HELP!" shook from my mouth, teasing her.

Tearfully, she reiterated, "HELP! I'm the one who needed help." She opened her purse, again, and pulled out a pack of tissues.

"You and some others," I reminded her.

"I was so ready to go."

"Why?" I had to ask. I knew the answer, but I wanted to hear it from her since she had brought up the topic.

Hard to believe that I would ask that question, appeared to have increased her adrenaline. "Are you serious, Devin?" Humored, Imani stared in disbelief.

"I'm only kidding, sis. You know me. I had to witness that expression on your face, again. Like old times."

"That's enough action to call it a night. Let's roll it back for a second. Imagine this. We all are having a good time—calm, cool, and collected. And all of a sudden, while running, somebody yells, 'SNAKE!'" Her eyes grew larger, the more she talked about it.

Staring at her innocent theatrics, I responded, "Absolutely hilarious." I had no problems following the script. She had created a perfect picture.

She added, "That reptile had crawled to the front where we were singing."

I couldn't help but say as I politely cut in, "Maybe, it liked what it heard, or, maybe, it didn't."

She suddenly laughed, and so did I.

"Umph," she grunted. "We didn't wait around to find out. We ran at a high speed."

"I'm sure you did."

"Never knew where it came from." Her eyebrows queried. "Regardless, I was ready to leave for another reason."

"Which was?"

"All we could think about was that the reptile's mother had to be somewhere around—close. Paranoid, I forgot why we were there in the first place."

"Umph." I shook my head. "As the saying goes, 'Get ready, pack your bags, and let's go!' "

Imani silently cried, wiping her eyes. She was too tickled to say another word.

Even I became emotionally crippled by this conversation. I wanted to laugh badly, once more, but I couldn't. I brought the conversation to an immediate halt. "I've had enough," I said as I raised my hand, surrendering.

The timing couldn't have been more perfect as I spotted our waitress. As requested, when we were seated, she brought two glasses of water, then took our orders. "I'll be back shortly," she said and swiftly walked away.

"Thank you," we replied, weak from all the emotional activity.

Although I was enjoying quality time with Imani, we were ready to change the subject. She had resigned, just as I had. Her eyes had turned red. Already she had two to three tissues balled up in her hand. Before saying another word, we picked up our glasses of iced water.

I drank a couple of swallows, then set my glass in front of me. I glanced at Imani. "Mom and Pop look well. And so do you," were my compliments, "even though your nose is red."

She slightly shook her head and blushed. "We have to keep up with you, Devin." Her smile was bursting with sunshine. "Mom and Pop are doing very well. They keep themselves busy and active."

I smiled, while touching the contour of the glass. "That's a good thing. I'm glad to hear that. Anything new? Because I know, when they get involved with something, they're engaged."

She leaned forward. "I will say this, and I can't say anything more."

My eyes were fixed on her as I met her halfway. "What would that be?" She now had my undivided attention.

"You are in for a surprise."

The suspense had me going. "Is it that you don't know more than you already know, or, is it that you have no plans on spilling the beans?"

Playfully defending herself, Imani raised both hands, palms up. "Honestly, I know very little. I'll leave that to them."

Her warm smile drew a lot of attention from where I sat, but, I decided not to push the issue. "Fair enough."

In the comfort of my hotel room, I had just taken a nice warm shower and put on my PJs and matching robe. I looked at my watch on the end table and realized that I still hadn't called Dr. Johnston back. I flipped the phone and waited for someone to pick up on the other end.

By the third ring, she answered, "Good evening."

It was plain that she was an orderly person. From my call earlier, I noticed her pronounced mannerism, yet, I detected a pure softness about her. Maybe, she had been in a delicate profession that had demanded her utmost attention and many hours of service at some point in time. From the sound of her voice, she had driven miles of experience in her lifetime and was well in age.

"Good evening, Dr. Johnston. This is Devin Fairchild. I hope I haven't called at a bad time."

"Oh, yeeees. Devin Fairchild." Without hesitation, she assured me, "Not at all. Quite frankly, young man, your timing couldn't have been better. I was just beginning to wind down for the evening."

Before I knew it, an involuntary smile surfaced. She sounded charged and refreshed, as if she had awakened from a restful sleep. "Good. I had thought maybe I should call tomorrow."

"I'm glad you called this evening instead."

"In that case, I'm relieved to know that." Not only was she glad that I had called, but I was anxious to know more about this lady and of the "promise" she must keep.

"It has been a very, very busy day. But, one other important business matter to take care of won't hurt anything, Mr. Fairchild."

Engaged, I held the phone tightly against my ear, listening intently, as she continued.

"Not only am I elated to speak with someone who sings my kind of music," I heard her say in the kindest voice, "but, I'm relieved to be able to have this opportunity to speak with you. Camille kept her word and acted quickly."

Feeling more relaxed about her introduction, I replied, "She's a good person. She made sure I received your message."

"And I appreciate her efforts. That sweet, young lady has been so kind, while trying to help me connect with a very special person. It is important that we talk."

...the beat held its breath...

CYMBALS

Cymbals are concave,
circular,
brass plates,
creatively made,
for its interesting role,
commanding attention.

It's a tinkling,
clinking,
or,
clashing,
brilliant sound—
oftentimes,
an intersection,
striking,
musical part.

Depending on the frequency,
unpredictably,
its high tones reverberate.
Like a chime clock—
when the bird sings,
everything stops!

…STOP!…Listen for the rain of music.

Chapter 12

NAN MOTHER

As I glanced at the clock and noticed that it was now 8:50 A.M., a bright light, like a reflector from a moving object, seared through the sheer panels. I walked to the living room window to inspect. When I looked out, I watched a vehicle pull into the driveway. Instantly, I smiled, not only at what sparkled from the outside, but also at who I knew to be on the inside. At last, I would finally get my chance to meet the fella.

"Well, he is prompt," I spoke out softly as I inspected the shiny wheels, too. The entire vehicle shimmered. He brought with him even more sunshine to the neighborhood. I wondered if that was what drew someone else's attention when I saw him waving. Then, I thought, *Does he know one of my neighbors?* From where I stood, I could not see who he was waving at. Not long after, I noticed someone with long hair and dressed in springy colors, walking along the edge of the street toward my driveway. The closer she came, the more I recognized her. The beautiful young lady, Camille, was headed his way. The tall fella met her halfway. While they exchanged words, I went into the kitchen and let my helpers know that our visitor had arrived. Shortly, thereafter, the doorbell rang.

I walked to the door as others followed to welcome our guest. It was evident that those behind me were ready to burst with excitement. I sensed an aura of alacrity coming from them. We were all elated to have this icon take time from his schedule to visit people who were foreign to him. As for me, I felt as though I had known him for a long time.

Mumbling coming from behind ceased when I opened the door.

"Good morning to you both," was my immediate salutation as I reached to unlock the glass door to let them enter. Just as if I had been wearing spectacles all along, the glass sparkled and glistened. I could plainly see the reflections of those who stood with me. The two visitors, along with Josie, Marcella, and myself, appeared as one big painted picture. We were brightly beaming just as the two that were standing outdoors. Their smiles were perfectly framed, and we had seemingly been juxtaposed as reflections, capturing the present moment.

"Good morning, ma'am," Mr. Fairchild said, standing behind Camille and appearing to be as tall as a professional basketball player. Although, I had seen men who were even taller, it never ceased to amaze me.

"Good morning, Nan Mother," Camille responded.

My fingers couldn't seem to unlock the glass door fast enough to welcome them in.

"Come on inside," I told them.

With open arms, I embraced Camille, just as if she had always been a part of this family. She had found a special place in my heart. She was someone I had become fond of in a short amount of time.

She, then, asked, "How is everyone doing this morning?"

Quickly, the responses came all at once from the rest in no certain order.

My reply trailed in last, purposely, to humor her and the young man. "I'm doing good now." My voice raised some octaves as I took off my apron.

My incendiary comment caused the bunch to erupt with laughter. A little old spice of humor never hurt. The effects loosened them up a little without any effort.

Camille placed her hand on my shoulder and decided to say next, "How about that? Finally, the person you'd been hoping to talk to is now standing right here in your very own living room. It can't get any better than this."

"No, it can't, dear. I owe many thanks to you."

"Not at all, Nan Mother. Anything for such a nice lady." Finding this the opportune time to move on to what was on her mind, Camille cheerfully and eloquently said, "Nan Mother, I know you both have met by phone, and I'm glad that you were able to finally connect. When I saw Devin drive up, I felt that I could, at least, escort him to your front door and formally introduce you both."

"Certainly, I don't mind that at all, dear. I like your style. Besides, I've already called Larry and Nancy for breakfast. I would like for you to join us, too."

She spread both hands then clasped them together, accepting my invitation, "Oh! Well, that sounds good to me."

"Wonderful. We would love to have you here."

Then, she glanced at the gentleman. "Devin," Camille proceeded, gesturing with one hand, glad to do the honor, "This is Dr. Johnston. Dr. Johnston, this is none other than the one and only Mr. Devin Fairchild." The joyride was all in her voice.

Eyes were shining from every direction. The young man had patiently been waiting to get a word in for himself.

He reached to shake my hand and nodded, "After only speaking to you over the phone, it's good to finally put a face with a name." He calmly chuckled. I guess finding the previous chatter a little comical, or perhaps a little nervous, but I had a feeling that nervousness wasn't a part of his character. He may have been confused about the reason for his visit more so than anything else. He remained calm and collected but very friendly and polite.

Agreeing with him, I uttered, "Yes, it is." However, glad to see him for a good and worthy cause, I didn't hesitate to say, while we were still shaking hands, "Well, you made it." With great satisfaction and relief, all I could do, at the moment, was nod my head, delighted that this day had finally come.

Smiling, he commented, "I'm here, and I see I'm in the right place with all these big pretty smiles." All of a sudden, he seemed to have batted his eyes in disbelief once he spotted Josie. I was curious to know what had triggered his reaction. It was almost as if cymbals commanded his attention with a clinking or brilliant clashing sound, reverberating inside his head. And if it was anything like that, the striking intersection served its purpose. Maybe, no one else had caught on, but I saw that something had railroaded his train of thought. Reminded me of a chime clock—when the bird sang, everything stopped!

Suddenly, Jay came from around the corner. "Have I missed something?" he asked enthusiastically. Then, he gustily headed toward Mr. Fairchild. The young boy seemed to have fire in his shoes. "Heyyyy, Maestro!" Jay greeted him, talking as if he had known the man of the hour for some time.

That tickled Josie.

That's my great-grandson...not afraid of company, I thought. Never had a shy bone in his body. If he had shown any signs of reticence, I would've been concerned. He knew just how to make others feel comfortable on contact.

Jay shook his hand with manpower in his grip. Likewise, Mr. Fairchild responded with just as much force. He gladly welcomed Jay's bold and friendly salutation.

Our guest chuckled, finding the teenager amusing and entertaining. He replied, "Hey, my brother."

They shook hands in a fashion that they apparently were accustomed to. It was one of those power shakes that only men understood, and, it didn't seem to bother Mr. Fairchild one bit. If I hadn't known any better, a person would have thought they were related. Jay's upbeat spirit became contagious, and that was just fine by me.

"I'm Jay. And, of course, I know who you are."

"I see!"

Jay chortled, drawing Mr. Fairchild and the rest of us into the net. The spirit of laughter consumed the place.

His mother glanced at me. She shook her head and smiled at our guest and said, reaching to shake his hand, "I'm Marcella, Jay's mother."

"Nice to meet you, Marcella."

"Excuse my son. He's normal," she got tickled again. "He has his own way of expressing himself."

"That's fine," he smiled, too. "It's an expression I'm familiar with."

"Mom," Jay began to explain his actions, "really…it's alright."

Often, I wondered where he got his theatrics. Certainly not from anyone I knew. On second thought, now, as I thought about it more, maybe, there was someone that was rubbing off on him—De. Or, maybe they were rubbing off on each other. However, Jay was good at it and sounded as though he was a physician, consoling a patient with the right pitch in his voice. Sometimes, I had to look real good to see if he was actually doing the talking. And this was one of those times I paid close attention and got a real good look at him in action.

He continued, "Males have a way of communicating. Isn't that right, my friend?"

Mr. Fairchild couldn't seem to stop smiling from all the attention. "Yes, we do," he vouched for him and, at the same time, enjoyed observing Jay's every move, most likely wondering what was next. This was maybe one visit that would be long lasting, all in good humor. I'm sure he hadn't expected, in the least, to be entertained nor detained by a teenager.

Jay moved on. "Hello, Miss Camille."

She returned the greeting, impressed, just as her friend. "Devin, you have an admirer here."

Mr. Fairchild reached for something in his pocket and handed it to Jay. "You're the Maestro. From what I've observed, I think you've something here. Here's my card. Call me sometime."

"Now…I like this young man," his admirer replied with the widest grin.

We all laughed, again.

He tapped the card, then put it in one of his pockets. With appreciation, he told him, "Thank you."

"My pleasure."

Next, I decided to introduce one last person, "And this is Josie, my great-granddaughter."

Once more, his face revealed that same puzzled expression. "Oh, yeees," he apparently remembered something. "I thought you looked familiar. You have some voice."

I hadn't heard silence that loud and clear in a long time. Every person in the room stared his way in bewilderment. I was sure they wondered just as I had, *When and where?* Some expressions were worth a million words, and, I was sure from the stunned looks on our faces, worth every penny.

"You've heard her sing before?" the young lady, Camille, asked him.

Mr. Fairchild had everyone's undivided attention. "I have," he answered. He smiled and commended Josie. "I had the opportunity to witness and hear your beautiful voice yesterday. I was impressed." He took a few steps in her direction to personally shake her hand.

Although surprised by what Josie had just learned from this widely known singer, she smiled and courteously said, "Thank you. That's a great compliment coming from you."

"The compliment is yours. You deserve it. I look forward to hearing more of where that comes from."

His friend, Camille, even appeared surprised. "You were there?" She had to be thinking the same thing, in more ways than one.

"In the audience?" I asked, softly, but yet with so much curiosity in my voice.

Camille kindly cut in, "That was my next question."

Our sudden line of questioning had tickled her, too.

His eyes beamed, which validated his answer, "Absolutely. I heard it all. You," he let Josie know emphatically, "the choir…and the minister. As I recall," he chuckled, "you hit those notes quite well."

We were in shock.

"As a matter-of-fact," he went on to express what was laid on his heart, "after the minister declared 'I'm enjoying this place I know,' you joined her and later took the floor. They picked the right one for the part. You are an outstanding cantor. You were great. I enjoyed every moment."

Josie blushed. "Wow," her voice trailed almost to a whisper. "You were there the entire time?"

"I got you on candid camera," Mr. Fairchild chuckled.

She knew he had to have been there from all the accounts he had just given on recall. The details were crystal clear, as if it was happening all over again. Quite often, she had been commended for her gift, but an applaud coming from this young man was one accolade she would cherish for life. As an artist of gospel music, he knew the road of this profession very well, and she realized that.

Marcella smiled at Josie.

Jay patted her on the shoulder. He was always in her corner. He held her in high esteem when it came to that, besides being a protective brother.

"Oh, my," I said, "I'm surprised neither of us saw you."

"Likewise," the fella answered. Obviously, he thought it to be a little odd himself. "The only person I saw is this young lady." If he thought as I had, it wasn't as if the place was as huge as mega churches these days. However, we weren't expecting anything out of the ordinary either.

Then, another question entered my mind, "Well, what brought you our way?"

"During our family reunion, over the weekend, some family members invited me to join them. We were sitting in the rear because the edifice was filled to capacity. I arrived just in time, before all the seats were filled."

"You must've left right afterwards?"

"Yes, I did."

"Well, that explains it. I'm glad that you enjoyed yourself."

He nodded. "Immensely, Dr. Johnston."

"Dear, just call me Nan Mother. You're family now and in the home where good people enjoy good people."

After saying that, I was ready to make my way to the dining area and say grace.

He chuckled. "I'd like that. And...you can call me Devin." He kissed my forehead, gracefully.

"Oh, Lawd. This is getting better and better." I laughed with everyone else.

Not long after, before anyone decided to strike up another conversation, I had to make just one announcement, "Well, now...I'm ready to hear some skillets and silverware. Yes...yes...yes." I nearly sang those three simple words. "And if we don't get our guests to the table soon, breakfast will be cold." I looked at them for some show 'nuff mercy because we had been standing in the same spot since Mr. Fairchild arrived. I certainly didn't want the young man to think we were from the Stone Age and didn't know any better.

"Now, that's what I'm talking about!" a voice said at the door, ready to claim a seat in front of a place mat.

…some orchestrations are dynamic
and worth a million words…

SHAKERS

Shakers are crafted,
to embrace and manipulate,
sounds by motion,
rhythm,
an expression of music.

Cleverly designed,
a shaker awakens,
to shake the deep,
massaging grooves,
etches in walls,
beyond windowpanes,
reaching cellars,
of the consciousness.

Isolated by its rhythm,
the rattle is mesmerizing,
perfect reactors,
mind chasers,
knocking,
to surmise,
what's held at bay,
behind sheets of fog,
murky gray.

...mind-stirring activators.

Chapter 13

CAMILLE

After Nan Mother said a brief prayer, while sitting at the head of the table, she went on to say, glancing at each of us, as we continued to hold hands, "I thank all of you for coming, especially our guests, Devin and Camille, who we are so delighted to have join us today after traveling from so many miles away. Family and friends are special and an honor to have. Whether family or not, I am thankful that all of our paths have met. Each journey has a purpose, and, presently, I am happy to be at the crossroads. As unique as we all are, we are refined by the choices we make, by the wisdom we cherish, the joy we spread, and the peace that sparkles from the beacons of our love. With these incendiary attributes that have been shown in my home today, it is my hope that these cherished links that have brought us together will never be broken. I, also, hope that our navigations will never be beclouded in this ever-changing world. Since we are chosen for our own destinies, I hope that we continue to have harmonious journeys that will surely bind us together along the way. I, Nan Mother, welcome you."

As she smiled and nodded her head, everyone released hands and thanked her in return.

De said comically and anxiously, "Nan Mother, I love you dearly and loved every word…you said. *Bless you. Breakfast is calling my name. Can we eat now?*"

Instantly, laughter and chatter filled the air as his parents shook their heads.

Tickled, Nan Mother answered dynamically, "Honey, I'm ready, too, and been ready ever since you knocked on the door. Now, will someone pass my boy there something to eat! Yes! Yes! Yes!" She swayed to her own musical words.

"Devin," his pop Larry said while passing a large platter of steaming hot spinach eggs his way, "I really can't blame you. The food smells delicious."

Hmmm, my mind jolted, *that is his name, isn't it? Hadn't heard it in so long, I had totally forgotten that "De" was only his nickname. Interesting. We have two Devins at the table.* From that thought, I couldn't help but glance at the other one sitting at the other end. He appeared to be surprised himself.

Nan Mother smiled. "Gracious, Lawd! We have two!" She looked at one and then the other. "That is right."

Everyone's eyes at the table shifted between the both of them.

"As a matter-of-fact," she continued, "you both look like you could be related." Because of their physical similarities, she had a point. Both were tall with fair skin and light eyes. And it wouldn't be long before De reached Devin's height.

"That's amazing," I had to agree. "What a coincidence."

Devin smiled at the youngster as he passed the platter of turkey bacon, "Looks like I have a twin."

"Mr. Devin," De reached for his napkin, "you have some big shoes to fill."

An outburst of laughter erupted since we knew that statement was wishful thinking.

Larry and Nancy looked at him as if to say, "Is he joking?"

I wondered who was more comical by nature, De or Devin. De's ongoing sense of humor came as a surprise, especially since I hadn't seen him in a while. By no means was he quiet or bashful. He knew how to entertain, which put him in the same rankings as his friend, Jay.

Devin couldn't resist chortling. "Do I, Little De?"

"You sure do."

"You definitely have to teach me a thing or two."

My Little De had me just as curious as everyone else. We all seemed to be wondering how he would respond. Although it was a compliment, he had to wonder what he could possibly teach someone who had already had plenty of experience in the industry. Not everyone had received that honor. However, not all professionals were as genuine as Maestro. In this instance, Devin probably was impressed with De's humor and intellect.

We soon found out that De's shoes weren't that large after all. He backed out, grinning, with a bowl of grits in his hand. "I'm only kidding, but I'm honored to have the same name as yours. Wait till my friends hear about this." He bobbed his head a few times like it was keeping beat to a rhythm somewhere deep in his mind.

With an interest, Jay told Devin, "I'll wear whatever size shoe you want me to wear, Maestro. Just show me what to do."

Josie snickered, and so did De.

Devin slightly shook his head, beaming, while stacking a layer of pancakes on his plate.

Marcella overheard. She had left and reentered the room with another platter. "Joshua…" she quickly got a word in, amused, but, at the same time, made sure she was careful as she placed more food on the table. She kept it coming until there was enough for the feast and then sat down to join us.

When I looked up as I passed the hash browns, my eyes landed on Devin and paused in mid-air. For some strange reason, he appeared to have seen, as one of Jarvis's famous lines, Casper the Friendly Ghost. His countenance spoke volumes, which he tried to immediately hide but was unsuccessful. I couldn't ever recall seeing his visage with grooves of wonder deeply etched in it. At least, not to this degree. On second thought, I had, as I remembered his puzzled expression at the mall. The previous day, it didn't seem as pronounced as the present. The indentures were so questionable that I discreetly looked in the same direction to see who had stolen his attention. His eyes, seemingly, were glued on Joshua, who I knew as Jay. *Umph,* was my next thought, *I wonder what startled him. It could be anything.* It was evident that he was deep in thought. *Maybe, he remembered something very important.* And I certainly hoped he felt all right. Soon after, he picked up his napkin and cleared his throat, then took the next platter being passed around. No one else seemed to have noticed, but I knew that he had taken an unexpected trip into wonderland whether it was personal or otherwise. When he realized that I was looking his way out of concern, he nodded with a kind smile, as if nothing had ever happened, just as Nan Mother responded to Jay's last comment.

"The young man needs a break, sometimes," Nan Mother gently admonished Jay, but, at the same time, she loved his spirit of entertaining their guests. "We don't want to put him to work; he may never come back!" Her eyes had enlarged just as the swelling of her comment sent us all rippling right back into laughter again. She kept us entertained, just as the younger ones, and I loved it.

Unexpectedly, after receiving the next dish, Maestro threw several musical notes our way that took us all by surprise. "I'll be back…" he smiled. "Excuse me, but, I thought I needed to show the lady of the house my appreciation."

Some silverware clanged from the shock, while others had their mouths gaped. The entire clan was stunned, but they weren't silent for long. A sudden outburst of elation erupted.

I shook my head but was delighted. Every drop of rain that came out of his mouth landed, softly, with a little lightning for emphasis, without any effort on his part. That shouldn't have come as a surprise since I had witnessed some of his most soul-stirring moments on several occasions. Whatever prompted him to improvise definitely lit a match under what was to come. Maybe, that was part of his plan. They got a chance to see just who he really was—down to earth.

Devin added, "You can count on it. How can I not? You have spoiled me already with this delicious meal, not to mention your generosity and kindness." Devin looked at Nan Mother sitting at the other end of the table with sincerity, still smiling, as if there was no other place he'd rather be at that very moment.

Nan Mother blushed. "I'm so happy to have you in my home, to grace us with your presence. If you only knew."

"I think I do. And I'm glad I came."

Devin smiled at me. I knew exactly what that meant. He, then, poured syrup over his buttered, hot pancakes, while others resumed and put their silverware to use. The aroma of maple traveled through the air, blending in with every other palatable dish that had been beautifully placed under our noses. The brown substance reminded me of lava gushing over a mountain. Its scent even smelled like a delicious inhalant.

With that said, I dug into my meal without delay, dipping squares of pancakes in syrup, ready to savor my first bite. This was the opportune time for everyone else to do the same before any other distractions arose, which was bound to happen. It had already been proven, so far, that

Nan Mother's guests not only enjoyed the meal but felt very comfortable in her home. And I believe that was exactly what she wanted, regardless of why she had invited Devin.

After some minutes went by, I realized that Devin and Larry were in a heartfelt discussion. With all the other chatter going on, which was very low, Larry conveyed to him, openly, "I tell you, man, you are a breath of fresh air for these younger ones here. I, myself, am glad you're here."

"I have to thank the Man Upstairs because my visit was not planned. Evidently, it was meant to be this way."

"Sounds like it to me."

Just as I sat my glass back down, I felt as though I was watching a commercial playing on mute. As if he had laryngitis, Jay released words to Devin that, apparently, impacted him. No one else seemed to have caught on but me. He did it so quickly and smoothly. As I had previously thought, it was bound to happen. Being as good as the inspector in the *Nancy Drew Mysteries*, I had a knack for cracking silent words.

Devin reached for his glass. "Not sure I understood you. Did you say—"

"I'm inspired," Jay told him quickly for the second time but spoke his words into existence loud enough for everyone else to hear. He had heisted the moment.

"That's what I thought you'd said. We have to talk. I'd like that. What do you say?" Devin took a sip of his orange juice.

"Sounds good to me, Maestro. I have your card."

De comically asked Jay, "What's your code?"

Beaming, he said, "Inspire!"

Nan Mother gently laid her silverware down.

Marcella stared at Jay with wonder.

At the same time, that was when I noticed, for the second time, a puzzled look spread across Devin's face. Something must've been trying to filter or compute in his mind. It was as if the craft of shakers had musically sounded off in his head. From what I had seen in musical renditions, hand shakers were rattlers that could be mesmerizing. Likewise, this same effect had an impact during quiet and unexpected moments. The swing in conversations seemed to have awakened something somewhere deep down, massaging grooves and etches behind his light eyes. The rhythm of rattlers had locked him in temporary isolation.

"You, Jay, really want to be a vocalist?" Nan Mother inquired.

"You?" Marcella chirped.

"Nan Mother," De gladly and enthusiastically chimed in, grinning, with a piece of turkey meat between his fingers, ready to bite down, "Jay and I, both, may be on that train."

"You got my vote," replied Larry, just as thrilled.

Nancy appeared speechless. As comical as De was, at times, a person just didn't quite know what his true feelings might have been. Although I hadn't seen him for some years, in recent times, he occasionally sent emails to let me know how he was doing. Academically, he was a straight-A student and had a knack for being creative. He loved to volunteer his services for various functions and was always very helpful at home. And he liked animals and loved sports. Very active for his age. But I never thought that he would entertain music other than wanting to someday sing in glee club. But now that I thought of it, Nancy did mention at the hotel the other day that De and her neighbors had entertained them. And I guessed I was looking right at the other two who were most likely the ones she was talking about. The thought had never dawned on me before then. Impressed, I glanced at the three of them and could only smile when Jay responded to both Nan Mother and Marcella's previous questions. Disbelief had settled way beyond the surface of their visages.

"Hadn't hit me before now. Never know," Jay shrugged, ready to put a spoon full of grits in his mouth.

"All I can say is, after that performance that you three put on the other day," the lady of the house stated, "doesn't surprise me in the least. You were good."

Devin seemed taken by the on-going conversation. He sat back and observed. Obviously, the two in question had his utmost attention. His eyes shifted between them. Josie, on the other hand, was no mystery. We all knew what she was capable of rendering.

"That's right," Nancy chimed in. "Larry and I saw a little of it ourselves. Although we couldn't hear very much, we got the picture."

Practically everyone around the table halted what they were doing when we saw what happened next. Josie laid her silverware down. She put her hands in her lap and, while smiling at Jay and De, began speaking politely:

> "I was inspired,
> by someone I admired,
> who shook the gravity of my life,
> looked into the depth of my being,
> finding a chest of jewels,
> hidden sparkles,
> opened by inspiration,
> for my flowers to grow."

Sounds of "hmmm, ummm, and umph," had circulated around the dining area as if we were judges for an audition or play. Intrigued, I smiled at the young lady's recital. No sooner had Josie finished when De chirped:

> "There's a purpose,
> why we live here,
> since the day we came,

to live our story.
Where's our next step
to advance with time?
That's why nothing remains the same—
not making a change
injects pain."

Nan Mother softly chortled as Marcella whispered something to her. With her sudden approval, she said, "Yes, we have a purpose. That's right!" She slightly waved the formal napkin that was gripped in her hand. If I didn't know any better, I would have thought we were sitting on the "amen" bench. Spontaneously and smoothly, Jay followed suit:

"I came,
with a code called "Inspire,"
through sunshine or rain,
through pain;
my arrival will not be in vain,
to give back to a life,
a paradise to frame."

"That's right," Nan Mother reiterated, emphatically, rocking forward in her high-backed chair. "Take us on back to the steps of freedom."

Immediately, chuckles escaped into the air, but she was serious. I had never heard that before and won't forget it anytime soon. Enthralled, we all were in a semi-trance as each of them took turns right after the other. Lastly, all three spoke in unison without flinching or stumbling as if they had had a pact since grade school:

"Even my schoolmates,
your inspirations are diamonds.
When they can't find the chest of jewels,

show them their hidden treasures—
inspire them to achieve their goals,
to find their desires,
sparkling in a cove,
to spread like fire.
An inspiration
that moves souls."

Instant chatter engulfed the room. As I glanced around the table, enjoying those who I had the pleasure of being in the company of, my mind traveled. Moved, momentarily I thought of Kathy and Paula. If they had heard them, they would have been impressed, too.

The way things turned out over the weekend had been joyous, positive, and heartwarming. And I had no regrets. Devin, on the other hand, I wasn't so sure about. Being the person that he was, he gave his admirers their accolades but, something just wasn't quite right. Now, I was convinced. Something had reached, most definitely, the cellar inside his brain, shaking his mind. The reactors were even tossing my thoughts around, trying to surmise the unknown. What was held at bay behind sheets of fog were murky gray. Wondering, I could only speculate. *Could it be that the mystery surrounding Nan Mother is beginning to weigh on his mind?* This was one of the most unusual situations I had ever seen. *What promise did she have to keep regarding someone she hadn't known?* He'd never know until those sheets of fog, which were so hard to navigate through for clear answers, dissipated.

...CAPTIVATING...

GUITAR

Six-string guitars,
are musical playgrounds,
to be creative,
producing desired sounds,
unearthing tunes,
with picks or fingers,
along its peculiar,
giraffe,
long neck.

Melting in its sail,
strumming to beats,
leave fascinating trails,
overflowing,
the mind's pail.

The art is timing.
Even when plucking,
the intensity is catchy,
mystical,
like sightings,
where tracks lay,
frames of evidence,
Milk Way.

…it's a galaxy of art in rhythm to the imagination.

Chapter 14

DEVIN

*U*mph, *umph, umph.* After seeing all that I had witnessed at the home of this beautiful lady, I was kept on the run mentally. *What is really going on?* was my next thought. Dr. Johnston and her family had made me feel so at home. Breakfast had been wonderful. The spread was setup and pleasantly decorated as something seen in gourmet magazines. Each complimentary item played its role. That included designer placemats with matching cloth napkins and plates. Every gold utensil, neatly placed for elegance, shone like new money. The classy layout impressed me. It would have been very difficult for anyone to ignore. Especially, a long table displayed with edibles that had the most enticing aromas attacking their olfactory glands. It felt like my sense of smell was on the verge of having a nervous breakdown. Someone with a lot of experience had made everything palatably satisfying and had cooked each delectable item to perfection.

The morning had been interesting and enjoyable. Being in the company of all those I sat with around the table was worth the time and was time well-spent. It hadn't taken long to get to know each of them in a most memorable way. Their styles were so personally welcoming, especially the youngsters, who showered me with their pure innocence. They were just being real in their own way. Josie, a captivating young lady, had put a spark in my heart. On her way to becoming a phenomenal vocalist, she had her own unique nature that could only bring out the best of her qualities. Jay and De, the duo who had kept me going practically from the time I had arrived, were…special. Like Josie, but in their own way, too. Although straightforward, myself, while entertaining in the presence of others, but, these youngsters ran with the ball of entertainment to home base with drive. And I admired them for that. They, too, had touched me in a special kind of way.

Even though stirred, I eventually became stunned by some of the things I had heard. From the shock, I felt sedated by something so strong that I was too confused for straight thinking. My thought process stuttered and tumbled. Now that I was sitting here quietly, all alone, I didn't know what to think. Dumbfounded as ever, I thought, *How could that—*

A voice took my thought away. "Devin." Larry came into focus as he returned and sat in one of the chairs on the front porch. "How long are you planning to be in Atlanta?"

Before I could answer, his wife, Nancy, came to the glass door and stood as Josie opened it for her. Carefully, she walked through with two glasses in each hand.

"Thought you both would like some lemonade."

Larry leaned forward in his chair and reached for the one she handed him. "Thank you, sweetheart," he smiled. "This is timely."

Appreciatively, I thanked her simultaneously.

"You're welcome."

Josie passed her the napkins, while still standing in the entryway.

"And here's one for you both. Enjoy," Nancy smiled.

"We will," Larry told her. He looked toward the door. "Josie," he said before they left, "thank you, too."

A gentle smile crept across her face. "You're welcome."

Josie held the door open as Nancy turned and went back inside where the ladies were clearing the dining area. We could hear dishes and silverware clinking. Nan Mother wasn't sure if my plans for the rest of the day were open or not, so, before her helpers got started, she thought she would ask, just in case. Since I still had time to spare until early afternoon, I let her know that she could take her time with whatever she needed to handle inside with the others. To humor her and, as a reminder of her earlier statement during breakfast, my exact words were, "I'm in no hurry to escape and never come back." Timing was in our favor, and I flowed with it.

Already, Larry and I had been chatting for the past thirty minutes, enjoying the moment. Even though we heard the sound of kitchenware coming from inside, we had not been distracted.

Larry turned up his glass and took a sip.

After I shook the ice in my drink, I answered, "Back to your question—I will be leaving tomorrow afternoon. The few days that I've been here have come and gone too quickly. Seems as though I just got here."

Following suit, I stole a swallow, too. The lemony and sweet-tasting drink quenched my thirst. The coldness made it just that much more satiating.

Larry shook his glass a little, seemingly enjoying the sound of ice cubes clinking. "I know what you mean. Sometimes, I feel the same way. One day, you're twenty-one and the next thing you know, you're thirty, then—"

I raised one hand and shook my head. "Whoa. You can stop, my friend. That's too much to think about."

He chuckled, and I did, as well.

My hand dropped to my knee, dismissing the thought.

He quickly glanced at me. "You married, man?"

I replied, "Not yet. Maybe, someday."

"It will come. You'll know."

"Maybe, I'll be as fortunate as you. From that smile you gave your wife, she has to be the best thing that ever happened to you."

"Nancy is great. I consider myself a blessed man."

To show my approval, I grinned and nodded repeatedly. "That's what I like to hear."

"Hopefully, when the right person comes along, she will be someone who is pleasant and just as entertaining as you are because, Devin, you lit this place up this morning with those other two, who kept you going."

My head fell back, smoothly laughing. He didn't even have to explain. I knew exactly the ones he was talking about. "It's been a beautiful morning, hasn't it?" I asked him, admiring the colorful flowers, shrubbery, and trees that lined Dr. Johnston's property line. Her turf had to be as green as a ripe watermelon.

As he gazed around the neighborhood, he answered, "I agree with Nan Mother. 'Good people enjoy being around good people.' Those are her famous words. That has been proven so today."

I agreed, "Yes, it has."

As we finished our drinks, we saw De and Jay briskly headed our way with a large dog on a leash. It had one of the largest heads that I had ever seen. It was a stocky, iron-built Rottweiler with a bandana around its neck and a cowboy hat on its head, secured with stampede strings. The dog trotted like a soldier. When that thought hit, I chortled in an undercover way, not wanting to offend his son. *What in the world?*

"I can just imagine what's going through your mind about now," Larry chuckled. He gazed at them not far away and made the situation even worse for me when he made a practical statement, "De, I'll give Midnight ten minutes, and that hat will be buried." He slightly shook his head. "Umph, umph, umph."

"Larry," my eyes welled up, "that's hilarious. Look at him—he knows he's in uniform. Now, that's a Kodak moment." I couldn't laugh like I wanted to, but, when I left, that was a different story. My stomach felt tight from the strain. For some reason, that scene, rolling before my eyes, reminded me of a comical show—*Gomer Pyle, USMC.*

He admitted, "That is hilarious. Some of these youngsters, these days, come up with some of the funniest things, but…that's De. On the other hand, I wouldn't want him to be any other way. He keeps us going."

"Yeah, you're right. I got a little taste of that earlier."

When they arrived, De replied, "I think he'll be all right. Isn't that right, Midnight?" He patted him on the back and then unsnapped the leash.

The dog looked up at him, and then stared at the football in his arm.

Jay said, "De, maybe, you should give him a snack. Your pop may have a point."

"Hey, Midnight," I looked at him from a distance, "I like that hat, man."

Before I could say another word, the dog took off.

In astonishment, everyone froze, staring at him as he galloped away.

De dropped the football. "Where are you going, Midnight?" His mouth lingered open as those words, instead of the ball, flew into the air.

Larry stood up and walked a few steps as he continued to observe. I got up and joined them, hoping this would not become a scene that required us menfolk to hunt him down. I was neither interested nor ready to work up a sweat.

The dog stopped abruptly along the side of the property lined with trees.

Great sighs of relief shattered the silence.

All of a sudden, he shook his head violently as he tried to remove the hat with his paw. It didn't take long before the hat fell to the ground. Swiftly, Midnight dug a hole in the ground. He was very animated. More so, on a mission.

"Looks premeditated to me!" Larry joked.

De and Jay laughed.

"You were right, Pop."

Jay darted to the far end of the yard and yelled, "Throw the ball, De! He'll run back!"

Good tactic, I thought.

"Yeah, that's right," De grinned. "He loves to play ball." Quickly, he took a few steps backward and threw the football upward.

Midnight didn't know it, but they had him under surveillance. As suspected, their plan worked. Distracted, he trotted toward the youngsters and sat on the sideline. He most likely couldn't wait to spring into action. That hat became history. At that moment, anyway.

Whew, the thought flashed. I was happy I didn't have to get involved. They had handled that well. Jay knew just what to do, especially at the right time, but that thought left when I heard an angel's voice.

The youngsters stopped to listen. They snickered and continued with what they were doing. Left totally in the dark by their reaction, I glanced at Larry, who was now looking toward the front entrance.

There stood Josie. She opened the door.

"Would you like more to drink?" Her eyes traveled between the both of us, smiling.

Larry shook his head. "No, thank you, but I appreciate you asking." He handed her his glass, and so did I.

"I'm fine," I let her know, "Thank you."

Once she left, a few minutes later, Marcella appeared at the door and said, "Nan Mother would like you both to join her on the back patio. If you would like to come through the house to get to the back, you're welcome to."

Larry and I responded that we would meet her shortly. We stood and decided on walking toward the back, instead. That alternative was timely. I had always been athletic and tried to stay fit as much as possible. Exercise was as important as the oxygen I breathed. However, my normal routine was, oftentimes, thrown off because of my hectic traveling schedule. When out of town on business, or, on vacation, that was another story. Time usually did not permit, and this was one of those exceptions, and I felt it. My muscles needed to be revived. They were beginning to ache. I slightly shook both legs.

Larry, then, rubbed and flexed one of his arms. "Umph," he said, "I know what I have to do before the day is over." Obviously, he needed some rejuvenation himself. "Exercise."

"Looks like we both need a little 'me' time," I chuckled.

"Yep, that's not even an option. That's exactly what I need. Your body definitely will let you know what time it is. Putting some weights on these arms will work that right on out."

Taking the long route had its benefits. Not only did the walk spring my legs back into action, giving them the workout they needed, but I also got to see the surrounding beauty of nature and her many rewards. Worth the saunter, I took it all in, since I was in an unfamiliar place.

When we made it to the back, we found Nan Mother, waiting with platters decorated with sweet-smelling fruit and other heartwarming edibles. She was in the perfect setting, while relaxing in a chair surrounded by an array of colorful food and accessories. It made her appear as though she had been placed on a tropical island. Deep in the South, she brought that fantasy to life. She had the best of both worlds right on her own back doorstep.

Still a little distance away, I heard Larry as he comically muttered, "Ooooh." At the same time, it appeared he was rubbing his belly for mercy. I didn't know if that was a sign of a bellyache or a hunger pain. As funny as it might have been, I held in my emotions.

Far from being removed from what we were tempted by, the smells of refreshments were trying to pound past the door of anticipation to get to my heart's desire. We were in for another round of indulgence, and she let it be known as we approached the table and sat down.

"Eat until your heart's content," she urged.

"What a spread," I smiled, taking it all in. There were a variety of fruits, cakes, pies, and an assortment of cheese and crackers displayed.

Larry joked, grinning, "You sure know how to treat a man, Nan Mother. Whew!"

She laughed herself almost to exhaustion, and I couldn't blame her because his emphatic statement had settled deep down in his voice.

He added, "I'm about to...pass out. But...I'm sure I have some room left. If not, I'll make room. Besides...I have to keep up with Maestro, right here."

"Well, my friend," I reached for a fork and said, "I'm ready."

"Let's go for it!"

Josie brought a bucket of ice with her and placed it on the table.

"Humph," Dr. Johnston said right before she asked, "Where are my boys?"

Josie volunteered, "They're in the front yard. I'll get them." She went back inside and closed the glass sliding door behind her.

"Everyone else should be out soon to join us. We know your time is limited," she glanced at me, "and, also, Camille says she has a flight to catch later today. I want to make sure everyone has plenty to eat."

I peeped at my watch. "You are generous. Thank you." I reminded her that I still had an ample amount of time left.

Not long after, Midnight ran from around the corner. He was running at top speed.

"Catch the ball, boy!" De shouted somewhere from the side of the house.

The dog was running so fast until it appeared he had no intentions of stopping anytime soon.

Silently, I hissed since I knew that thought was just an illusion. They could stop abruptly, almost as cleverly as the Roadrunner.

"Run, Smokey, run!" De egged him on.

Whaaaaaat, the word slammed in my head. *Smokey*, I heard myself say, silently, with greater confusion. *I know I'm not hallucinating.* I glanced at Larry.

"Did he call him…Smokey?" My eyebrows rose. I had to ask.

After gulping his drink, he answered, "Yes, he did."

Now, my eyebrows knitted. The timing of each mysterious incident was turning out to be a work of art that had been carrying me, psychologically, up and down, on a roller coaster. From the way this was going, the growing intensity shook my mind to the core. As if a guitar was musically plucking intensified notes and tones inside my head, it had unearthed spellbinding sounds I couldn't quite absorb. The several picks that I heard were so mystical and catchy, I needed some clarity, "I thought—"

Larry politely cut in, "De calls him Smokey because he's so quick."

He watched the onset as I did. Midnight retrieved the ball and trotted toward De. He snapped the leash around his neck and secured it around a tree.

"Oh," I understood, feeling the crease in my forehead relax. "That's his nickname."

Larry quickly looked in my direction. "Yes, his sobriquet." He pierced a slice of cantaloupe with his fork. "That's De!"

Concerned, Dr. Johnston asked, "Are you all right, dear?" Apparently, she had noticed the exposures of my various expressions.

Satisfied that the burning question had been answered, I replied, nodding, "Yes, I'm fine." Although I was puzzled, I had to keep that concealed. Who would ever believe the reason why I inquired? Some things were just meant to be left alone. Besides, it was a long story, one that I had not revisited for some time. *What a coincidence!*

Before I could think about any other mind-boggling chain of events, I was distracted when the glass sliding door opened. Laughter spilled into the air when the others came from inside.

De and Jay were soon to join us, too. They were in a serious rush when I heard Jay tell De, "Follow me, cub, to the well."

"How far is the well?" De asked him.

I stopped eating and went into a trance. *The well? What well? They have wells around here?* Thrown for a loop, I couldn't imagine the idea of anyone using one for the same purposes that people did in the early 1900s. *In the city?*

Jay replied, "From here, about half a sweet potato pie away."

Whaaaaaat, I thought for the second time within the last couple minutes. From the shock, I felt as though I had been electrocuted. I hoped I hadn't blown my cover. Although others were humored in their own way, I had chortled out of disbelief. And no one knew why. I really didn't know what to think. The next thing I thought was, *Am I dreaming, again?* I wondered if I would awake, at any moment, at home in my comfortable bed. I blinked a couple of times, but the setting had not changed. One thing I did know for sure—the film was rollin'.

I glanced at the two youngsters, again.

De chuckled, as if he had heard that statement coming from Jay many times before. He seemed to enjoy his pal entertaining him, passing the time away.

Amused, as they passed by, Dr. Johnston overheard, too. "Jay," her voice elevated slightly but gently, "are you still telling De a fairy tale about a well on this property being used in the twenty-first century? You're keeping the past alive, aren't you?"

The topic of their conversation had everyone's immediate attention.

"Someone has to, Nan Mother, but I'm glad those days of filling buckets are gone."

"So am I," she agreed, tickled. "And I can't blame you for that one, dear. However, private wells still exist, even in metropolitan communities, but that's a topic rarely talked about. And there certainly isn't one on my land in this day and time to be specifically used for my every need, but, back in the day, it was necessary."

De commented, "Can you imagine walking that distance…just to get some water?" Clowning, he shivered at the thought of it.

Trying not to be obvious, I shook my head, grinning, while chewing on a slice of honeydew melon and thought, *I've heard that one before.*

Comically, he added, "I would send Midnight!"

Laughter erupted. That was one scene I would have paid to see. Just like he had taken off galloping with great speed to bury that hat, he would—

"Come on!" Jay gripped him by the neck, playfully, then let go. "Let's go wash our hands because that's the sweet potato pie I'm talking about," he glanced at the table, "right over there."

Instantly, Dr. Johnston looked from left to right. "Where's Josephine?"

My ears burned. *Who is Josephine?* A sudden rush washed over me. I blinked twice, again. The film was still rollin'. I sunk deeper and deeper into thought. All the other striking incidences came reeling back, too. Confused, I targeted those frames of evidence where sightings of tracks laid etched in my consciousness. The signs warranted me to examine them closely. While speculating about bits and pieces, I, soon, visualized a Milky Way that had formulated beneath the roof of my cephalic dome. If my suspicions were correct, I could understand why the stars were twinkling. Still uncertain, I returned to the most recent frame, again. *Who is Josephine?* Then, it hit me. *But...then...maybe not.* Instead of any further contemplation, I let it simmer. Although, I had to admit—the similarities were equivalent to a strummer strumming to beats that were catchy. Felt like my mind swayed, left to right, melting in its sail, the more I thought about all that had transpired. *I like that beat. Nice.* It left fascinating trails, memories that overflowed my mind's pail.

...how ironic the beat...

HOW GREAT THE SOUND

Tic-toc,
at the dock,
the cradle rocks,
as mysteries unlock.

Ranging high and low,
pitches precipitate,
note by note,
as it undrapes,
clue by clue,
undeniable traits.

Like a symphony,
in living color,
it's captivating,
lingering,
forever so new,
indelible imprints,
landing,
on the ocean blue,
the landscape of the consciousness,
prancing,
from the depth of the owner's shoes.

…Who owns these melodies?

Chapter 15

NAN MOTHER

"Oooh, this has been just a lovely day," I commented with great satisfaction.

"O-o-o-o-o-oh," Jay amused me, "and it's not over yet."

"Lawd, child, what are you talking about?"

"Nan Mother," De said sincerely, which concerned me, "have you forgotten?" I couldn't remember the last time I had heard him speak so seriously.

Taken, more so by the abstract side of his personality, I asked, "Forgotten? Forgotten what, dear?" Now, the inquiry really chiseled at my curiosity.

Everyone stared at me with great wonder, except Devin and Camille.

My mind raced. "Would someone please tell me what it is that I have forgotten?"

All nicely in a row, starting with Marcella, she stood and surprisingly said, "Happy Birthday, Nan Mother!" She smiled.

When I saw that Jay was about to say something, I decided to wait before I spoke what was on my mind.

He stood up. "Happy Birthday, Nan Mother!"

This went on until each of my family members and neighbors had taken turns and stated their celebratory slogan in an orderly fashion. They had an impressive operation in motion.

Devin followed their lead, smiling. "I might as well join in." He kept the slogan going, then passed it on.

Camille fell in line last, delighted to be a part of the unexpected plan. She politely nodded her head gracefully with her hands clasped together when she spoke.

Even the dog stood up, staring as if he had been commanded to stand on guard. I guessed that he wondered what was going on.

Chuckling, I decided now was the time to get a word in. "Yes, it is on tomorrow. Happy Birthday to me!"

They laughed.

"With so much on my mind lately, I hadn't thought about it in the last few days. That's very thoughtful of you. I won't forget this day. Just…lovely. Thank you."

"YOU'RE WELCOME!" they chorused.

And before I could get another word out, my train of thought was severed.

"It's not over yet," De reminded me, enthusiastically, while eyeing his cohorts.

If my expression had shown what I felt, at that moment, they would have known that I was bewildered. *What is this young fella going to do next?*

All of a sudden, De, Jay, and Josie leaped away from the table and onto the lawn. With so much energy, they jet streamed to a perfect spot where they felt comfortable. They lined up in a straight plane, and then turned a couple of times in both directions.

I turned in my chair.

Surprisingly, everyone else followed to join them.

Totally lost and not really knowing what to do, Camille and Devin sat back down in their chairs and watched. Just as I had done, they chuckled, then laughed at the older ones, trying to repeat the same moves. They turned and turned, but slower. I supposed that they were trying to keep from getting dizzy. And, quite frankly, I couldn't blame them. Those youngsters had so much energy; I had to raise up in my seat.

Not a bit surprised, Larry playfully wiped his hand across his forehead. He glanced at his wife, motioning next to him and shook his head. She laughed at him.

The youngsters shifted gears on them as they stepped sideways, to the left then right, clapping their hands. Well organized, those three never missed a beat. They led the way:

"It is your birthday todaaaaay,
It is your birthday alwaaaaays,
It is on Sunday,
It is on Monday...."

Devin clapped with them. "I like that!" he chimed in with them, impressed, once he had gotten the hang of it.

Since the rhythm had a swingy, skippy beat, during their performance, all I could do was pat my feet. Captivated from the onset, my lawn became a stage floor with the sun shining bright on them. It wasn't long before the others caught on and were doing good themselves, with the exception of one. Larry rendered more theatrics than he could handle. He stumbled off course a few times before he mastered it perfectly. De, Jay, and Josie were a musical match. Good control. They had learned their roles very well. The more they sang and clapped, the more energized they became. When they finally decided to add more color and spice to their act, Josie rolled out both of her arms and raised them high in the air. Rolls of long, colorful streams were waving through the air as she turned in both directions. De and Jay turned once, simultaneously, right after her in coordination—march style—then moved as if they were ice skating in full stride.

"Umph," I said, amazed. "They didn't even miss a beat; they're on time. That's clever."

I couldn't imagine the rest of them even attempting to repeat all those different moves. But they did. Surprisingly, they succeeded. And Larry did not make one mistake.

I clapped for them, bubbling over.

Intrigued, Camille smiled, tickled. "That's what I call…a dynamic achievement."

"Look at him go!" Devin pointed in Larry's direction.

I understood Devin's point exactly, since Larry, somehow, stood out above the rest in good humor. Animation had never appeared this colorful to me, in more ways than one, in such a long time. From the serious expression on his face, he had to be concentrating very hard to keep up and remember what he was supposed to do. Marcella and Nancy, on the other hand, hung in there. They were on each side of him and that had to have been very difficult. I wondered how long all of them could hang on because Larry had them all on the edge of laughter. And that would have just thrown everything off. The youngsters couldn't help themselves; they had to get a sneak peak in whenever they could.

Devin looked my way and said, "They're good. I believe there's more where that came from." He appeared intrigued himself, specifically honing in on those leading. "Interesting."

As far as I was concerned, they had done extremely well, putting their best foot forward. And, De, Jay, and Josie couldn't have done it any better. For the very first time, my great-grandchildren and my boy from next door showed me a side I had not seen before. They were just as good as any other histrionics I had witnessed. "Just look at them…"

The day was still young—high noon. Jo-Jo had, once again, been fired up in my home. Sitting comfortably in the family room, her voice melted the silence, adding a shroud of tranquility throughout. The sounds from her vocals were silhouettes that shadowed her own voice to each awakening beat, sailing toward what I often called "Meditation Island." Although it had only been a day or two ago, it seemed as though I hadn't listened to her voice soaring in perfect harmony in a while. Technically, I hadn't, but keepsakes were just as good to have when I could no longer see what I had once seen live before my very own eyes. Those were the days.

Back then, Jo-Jo was one of my closest friends. How could I ever forget that one Sunday afternoon when she and I were at a restaurant back home? Like a symphony in living color, I recaptured unforgettable memories. As we sat at the table, we ordered one of our favorites—ice cream sundaes. We looked forward to those weekends. Routinely, we would stop in just to sit and chat, after leaving from off the glory bench. While we sat there, enjoying our cold, tasty treats, a fashionably dressed, clean-cut and polite man and pleasant woman approached our table. I'd seen him before but never really knew who he was until then. Jo-Jo didn't seem surprised, but she certainly was astonished when he offered her a business proposition.

I whispered, so I thought, to her my famous words, "Jo-Jo, whatever you do, don't forget the glory bench."

I was only looking out for my friend. Her eyes shifted and darted back in their direction. Before they walked away, the conservative and impressive woman smiled, then told her, "And we want you to remain on the glory bench."

I glistened. Not too many months later, Jo-Jo aired on the radio. Later, I found out that the proposition benefitted a good cause. She spoke and sang to children with disabilities who couldn't go, at will, to hear words of inspiration. So, she took it to them. There by her side, Jay even inspired her just that much more. While growing up as a much younger girl, I would have never thought of her in that role. *JO-JO?*

While reminiscing, my mind tic-tocked at the dock where flashbacks were importing and exporting. The cradle rocked, revisiting that scene vividly, once more. Seems as though I was sitting right there, again, at the table with her. No matter what time of day, the place always smelled good. Some atmospheres were not fitting for some occasions, but the country food blended well with the setting. What stood out the most were those plastic red-and-white-checkerboard tablecloths that made the place cheerful. I hadn't seen that anywhere else since, other than on one of those television shows later through the years. I could feel a smile slowly creeping across my face as I thought of that bell that rang every time someone entered that door. And how could I not remember that statue. My thoughts stalled as my eyes batted. *Of course*, I realized something that made a whole lot of sense, *that Mohawk Indian with the spear…* The pitch of the sound of what ran through my mind was ringing high and low as they precipitated. My head fell back against the chair, softly laughing.

"Umph, umph, umph," I heard myself mumble while shaking my head. Note by note, those pitches in my remembrance undraped clue by clue. They were undeniably traits of the people I loved. *Well*, my mind continued to churn, *if that's the case, then I may be able to narrow down who sent those posters*. And I didn't have to think for very long. If it was who I believed it was, then I knew exactly who had sent them. I felt almost positive and thought, *What a pleasant surprise*. I was glad the cradle had rocked as mysteries unlocked. Now, I could stop wondering.

That Fed-Ex delivery had baffled me the entire weekend. All that I recapped was orchestrated right on time. So real. Trails of the scene still lingered, forever so new, the memorable imprints of my two loved ones. Some recaptures were not as impacting as others, but this reflection was special. So much so that their indelible indentations were captivatingly landing on the ocean blue of my mind, right on the landscape of my consciousness. They often came reeling back, prancing, from the depth of the owner's shoes. *I cherish those days*, I thought. *The history and shoes of*—

"Nan Mother," Jay startled me as he entered the room with Devin from the patio, "Maestro is here."

"Oh, good," I glanced at the clock. "Time is passing quickly. That's how it is when you're having a good time."

Mr. Fairchild agreed, "I can attest to that. Jay and I were just having a quick, one-on-one chat."

"We have to do it again, Maestro." Jay shook his hand. He appeared as though he had not broken out in a sweat all day. Instead, he looked refreshed.

"Would love to."

Before Jay made an exit, he asked, "Do you need anything, Nan Mother, before I leave and join De? If so, would you like for me to get it now?"

I smiled. "Dear, it's kind of you to ask. There is one thing you can do for Nan Mother." As I remembered something very important, I took him up on the offer, even though I knew he would do whatever I requested. "There's a box in my bedroom. It is against the wall behind the quilt stand. Do you mind getting it for me?"

Offering his assistance, he responded, "One box, coming up." He briskly left the room.

Ready to turn my attention to why I had invited Mr. Fairchild, I proceeded, saying, "Please join me." I gestured for him to sit in a nearby chair. "Make yourself comfortable."

"I would be glad to. And hope it won't be the last," he humored me.

"I look forward to doing this again, especially since our paths have now crossed."

Devin respectfully nodded in agreement. "And, so do I."
Then, he admitted, shaking his head. "I have to be honest
with you. At first, I was reluctant to get in contact with you."
He gazed at me with the biggest smile, as if he could hardly
believe it. "When I first received the news from a friend that
someone he had no clear information about wanted to make
contact with me, I was a little nervous. I had no idea, at the
time, who you were. Although...I'm still at a loss, I'm glad
that I decided to come."

"For such an unusual request, I'm glad that you came
and have no regrets."

Behind his light eyes, his frozen stare appeared as
though that thought still hadn't quite filtered. If it hadn't, I
couldn't blame him, but, if so, something got his attention.
"That lady," he switched topics simply because he couldn't
quite put his finger on who had distracted him.

I listened. "Oh, yes," the voice overshadowed the present
conversation. "That's my Jo-Jo." Taking in the quality of her
gift was like a breath of fresh air. She mastered it like art
that had a substantial price tag. The brushstrokes of her voice
flowed with very fine details. It was a craft brought to life.

"Sounds like the same voice I heard a little earlier while
Larry and I were sitting out front. Only heard her for a brief
moment."

"She has an amazing voice."

Impressed, he almost whispered, "How great the
sound..."

Approving, I nodded to his complimentary assessment.

Between the fine line of reality and fantasy, Devin's
mind seemed to wonder far into the distance. I couldn't help
but notice a pattern of rhythmic beats flushing through the
surface of his being. He slightly rocked like a ticking clock
while raking in every note. It wasn't long before he snapped
out of his current mode of isolation and said with a humble

smile, "Her vocals are stunning. She's good and plays them well."

I was tickled by his last comment. "Maestro, that's a good way of putting it. Hadn't heard it put like that before. Joe—"

Jay quickly walked in with the box, breathing a little laboriously.

"Thank you. You can set it next to Devin." I, then, looked at Mr. Fairchild and told him, "It may be somewhat heavy."

He showed mixed emotions. Although bewildered, he warmly smiled and stared at it. He had to wonder, in his confused mind, what was inside and who it was from. He lifted the box to confirm its weight, then put it back down on the floor. "It's not too heavy. Thank you."

"You're welcome."

He further observed it, noticing the word FRAGILE stamped multiple times in red ink.

Not wanting to prolong his curiosity, I told him, "An explanation is in order. You have to be extremely puzzled about now."

"I am," he paused, "surprised."

"I know you are. You have been welcomed into my home by people you know nothing about, and now you're presented with a big box…" I softly chortled with the honor of fulfilling the promise I had made. "Whew," I felt relieved and was happy and ready to fill him in on the information he may have found to be even more surprising. "I'm glad this day has finally come."

He listened intently, waiting to hear what I had to say. His eyes said it all; they were fixed with suspense.

I continued, "What's in that box, right there, has seen many days. Jay wanted me to pass this on to you—"

Before I could finish, he asked, baffled, "Your little Jay? Your great-grandson?" I don't believe the poor man even blinked once.

"Umph," I wanted to laugh, but I decided not to. Instead, I said, "I know you're greatly confused, and I'll explain. I'm speaking of Papa Jay, who I also called 'Joe'. He was my closest friend and my husband. Little Jay inherited his first name."

"Ooooh," he immediately said. Inside his head, I knew his mind had begun to tick-tock.

"You knew Mr. Johnston?"

His eyebrows furrowed. "Mr. Johnston?" he pronounced slowly, sounding more puzzled than before. "Your husband…"

To put an end to the suspense, my eyes scrolled to one of the family pictures on the shelf.

"Joshua…"

...Whaaaat? Rewind that beat...

SAXOPHONE

Just as a perfect carving,
a saxophone is a conical metal piece,
dressed in brass,
dazzling like gold,
noted for its pure skin,
a sight to behold.

It's sleek,
a musical generator,
formed to be unique,
modulating,
historical freight,
glowing serenades,
heavy weight.

By musical servings,
its breathtaking eloquence,
magically flows,
with new revelations,
more proof,
chanting,
down its curvy spine—
a chance,
once more,
the spoken to dance.

…pure elegance.

Chapter 16

DEVIN

Waaaay behind cobwebs, my doorbell started ringing. The mystery of sounds was at it again, drumming up just as much suspense as before, playing on my consciousness. First, four bass notes were pounding and reverberating from my crib. Mysteriously, drum rolls came, twirling me into greater confusion with a sudden...pause. Next, a guitar picked intensely, then strummed. *Now, what?* I couldn't think clearly. I tried to figure out who this mystery person actually was standing on my doorstep. Aloud, I articulated, "Joshua Johnston?" Then, came a knock in my head; it had clearly jolted me. The words tumbled from my mouth, "You're Joshua Johnston's wife?" Purely stunned, my eyes finally trailed in the same direction as hers.

"I am," Dr. Johnston answered, tickled, "Genesis Johnston."

A sudden rush came over me. "From...Oklahoma?" I asked, still in shock, not expecting her to answer the obvious. Taken by this revelation, her response went into slow motion. The anticipated answer rang loudly, diminishing the silence. She smiled and nodded as she stood up and walked toward an array of photos displayed on multiple shelves.

Marcella walked in and met her at the path. I, on the other hand, had difficulties filtering the information. The process took its time, sifting through my hourglass. I found it hard to believe that I had been surrounded all morning by a past I had locked away as a keepsake not so many years ago. My eyes shifted to her, thinking, *Is that the Genesis whose pop had asked me to stop by their home? Could she really be Mr. Bailey's daughter? Is this really the daughter he wanted me to help in any way?* From what I remembered, Genesis snapped out of her trance when my voice shifted. If she only knew, that wasn't an act. She really thought I was an actor. *Umph*, I felt warmth inside. Those thoughts made me smile within. That was some kind of dream. *How could I ever forget it?* I often wondered what could have been in that tea I drank. That had to be one of the most powerful smooth teas yet. When I shut my eyes on that flight, I set sail for what seemed like days.

Whatever Dr. Johnston and Marcella were discussing was mute. Marcella's entrance could not have been timelier. Soon after, my vision became a blur. In suspension, I temporarily drifted. Rocketing to the past, it wasn't hard for me to reflect on that dream… *Immediately, I began to see scenes flashing as they came into focus at the sound of another apparatus on the loose. A sleek music generator, dazzling like gold in its pure skin of elegance, blended in at the perfect moment. The sax. Produced by the hands of my ticking brain, it had climbed altitudes of defining notes to accommodate and assist my thought process. They lingered and glowed. At the same time, the script was muted, as I saw various frames of people in motion. The only sound in progress was the music modulating in my head, keeping up with the transmission of what had come across. All of a sudden, like a radar, I spotted it. There it was—one specific scene in the midst of all the others that oscillated. The one of interest, that I had pulled up on recall stopped…right on time, as the saxophone whined. Just as its perfect carving, the debut took on a shape of music that was memorable to behold. Smooth and suave moves. The skill of each musical serving, which magically flowed, spilled its breathtaking eloquence throughout the regions of my mind. Purely formed to be unique, in rhythm to the mold of their destiny, there sat Genesis, still as a statue, in front of the window. She had long hair, was dressed in pink. A very beautiful girl. I could see why Mr. Bailey asked me and the others to come by. Why had she withdrawn? That was probably one question I'd never know the answer to. Besides, that part of the dream may not have actually happened. Humph, the composition of music began to speak, tickling my memory reserves. The dormant past news came like an informant, chanting, down its curvy spine. That was right! Ms. PeggyAnn had mentioned that incident. I felt a spring of elation as the spiraling, high pitches from the sax came and left in a zip. It had happened. That was not my imagination… Lastly, the piper whispered the last note.* My eyes flickered when I heard Dr. Johnston's voice reeling me in, back to the future.

"Maestro, are you all right?" she stared, with a couple of frames in both hands. As the seconds grew, she began to show signs of concern when her countenance became more serious than I had ever seen.

"Oh, yes," I tried to snap out of it without going into detail. "I'm fine. I…" I couldn't seem to focus fast enough between the past and the present. *Is this real?* What a question to ask myself seeing that the evidence stood right in front of me, several feet away.

She, then, asked, "What is it about Oklahoma that sent you hurdling into a daze?"

Astonished, I looked at her for a second, then smiled. I saw the little girl Genesis through her eyes. She seemed to be smiling gently my way. *It is her!* Those words dashed across my mind. Convinced, a wave of laughter hit me. "Honestly…it's a long story, but it's all good."

"Excuse me, young man. Josephine!" Dr. Johnston called out with a sense of urgency in her voice. She walked back to the chair and reached for her glasses that sat on a nearby table.

"Huh!" I uttered in sudden disbelief under my breath but managed to play it off well. I wondered, *Who in the world is Josephine? That's the second time I've heard that name.* With all the distractions earlier, I'd had no time to further entertain the thought. Only assumptions had consumed my global hemisphere. Technically, the only Josephine that I knew of was Joshua's sister. Oddly, I hadn't seen her yet.

Josie came quickly into the room.

My eyes shifted between the both of them. Deep inside the hollows of my mind, the silent words echoed, *I don't believe it. That's Josephine?*

"Will you bring the maestro a glass of iced-cold water for me? You and Jay can move a lot swifter than I." She sat back in the chair.

Josie softly answered, "Of course, I'll do it for you, Nan Mother. I'll be right back."

"Thank you." Dr. Johnston put on her glasses to get a closer look. I guess to make sure her eyes weren't deceiving her. "Just want to make sure you're all right," she smiled with a warm gaze.

"Thank you, but really, I'm fine," I assured her. "I just had a flashback. You reminded me of someone." A short but sweet rendition of the past had taken my mind away. Enthralled, I welcomed history, a chance, once more, for the spoken to dance.

Her smile slowly diminished. Apparently, something had dawned on her. "You mentioned Oklahoma. How did you know?" she asked with an interest in knowing since she personally had not shared that information with me.

Knowing that the details of how I had met her would only complicate things, I replied, instead, "A few years ago, I met a beautiful lady and dear friend by the name of Ms. PeggyAnn—"

Elated, she politely cut in, "Just want to be sure, but are you speaking of PeggyAnn from Oklahoma?" Excitement danced in her voice. And I could understand why. From curiosity, she sat more erect than before.

"Yes, that is her," I didn't hesitate to say. "Seminole County, Oklahoma."

Dr. Johnston's head fell slightly backward as she smoothly and warmly chuckled. "That's my friend, also. Isn't she a great lady?" Her eyes beamed.

Josie returned, holding a tray that held glasses of water and lemonade.

Dr. Johnston said appreciatively, "Thank you, Josie Rose. You always seem to surprise Nan Mother in one way or another." She reached for the glass and a napkin, and so did I.

"Thank you, little Josie." Since I was confused, I asked, "Or, should I call you Josephine? Or, would you prefer Josie Rose?"

Amused that I had inquired, she couldn't help but smile. "It doesn't matter. I like all three."

"I can see why you would be confused," Dr. Johnston stated. "Legally, she's Josephine. I have the privilege of calling her Josie Rose. Starting with my daughter, then my granddaughter, Marcella, it has been a tradition and an inheritance as their middle name. We call my great-granddaughter 'Josie' for short and 'Rose' as a sobriquet. She has the same name as my sister-in-law, which is Joshua's sister, Josephine. Both will be long remembered. As a matter-of-fact, that's Josephine singing now."

We listened, momentarily, as she delved into her iced-cold drink.

Amazed by the news, I said, "Jo-Jo is Josephine?"

That came as a bolt of lightning, as the same imaginary instrument as before, chimed in, too. Once again, it spiraled, artistically, reinforcing the proof of this lady's historical freight. Stirred, the striking fragment of tunes and tones pumped through my veins effectively. Well executed, it happened in just a matter of seconds and was gone without a trace.

"That's 'THE Josephine'," she let me know, tickled. Her acknowledgement sounded as though she could hardly believe it herself. "That's her."

All this time, I'd had no idea it was her we had been listening to. Neither, had I expected to be surrounded by two of them: one in person and one streaming through surround sound. She had no inclination what had really triggered my emphatic response. Since I couldn't believe it myself, I had to splash a gulp of water down my throat. If only she had known what had been locked away in my treasure chest for the past three years. From what I had just heard her say, I took another journey. Another segment of the dream came into full view as Dr. Johnston continued to listen, while consuming more of her drink... *Slowly, I heard the sleek horn stunningly bringing on the next set of glowing serenades. At the same time, I thought of how the Josephine that I knew very well had her own unique personality and was known for her comical ways. I could vividly visualize her with her brother Joshua. They both were entertaining when I had first met them. I couldn't help but zone in on her character. After getting a glimpse of each of her scenes, I had the joy of letting the strip of film stream. Learning that Josephine had became a singer later in life took me by surprise; I had not expected her dynamics. Ms. PeggyAnn animatedly expressed her approval about her capabilities, but I had no idea she would sound so amazingly beautiful. Knowing her as a teenager, I would have never thought she would, someday, blossom as she had. That realization took a moment to funnel through as I listened to the heavyweight of music that shone on the depth of her shoes. She's deep,* that thought radiated, while scrolling by when everything faded. *Incredible.*

Dr. Johnston recaptured my attention when she set her glass of lemonade down, humming. She picked up the two picture frames that were in her lap.

"These are photos of a young Joshua and Josephine."

As she handed them to me, I set my glass down and leaned forward to grab them. They looked a little older, yet they looked very much like themselves as teenagers, just as they had in my dream. When I had last seen them, they were well seasoned in age. Although, I hadn't looked at any of the clippings that Ms. PeggyAnn had given as keepsakes in a while, they were definitely the same individuals. I shared with her, saying, "I have clippings of your husband and Josephine from when they were younger."

Dr. Johnston appeared a little surprised and said, "Do you?" Her sparkling eyes pleaded behind her glasses for more information regarding her loved ones. I sensed that those closest to her were one of her favorite topics of discussion.

"Yes, I do," I nodded as confirmation. "Three years ago, they were given to me here, outside of Atlanta, at a nursing home and rehabilitation center. That was during the time when both had arranged for me to perform in the presence of Ms. PeggyAnn—"

"Oh, yeeees," she inclined her head, while responding, "I remember. I regret I was unable to make it, but they told me all about it." When she smiled, her entire face lit up.

To further fill her in, I continued, "The next day when I went to visit Ms. PeggyAnn, we had a nice, long chat. Before I left, she gave me the clippings. That was also during the time your husband left her a box for me. I was honored and totally surprised that he wanted to pass on to me his hat of inspiration."

Although, I now understood where De, Jay, and Josie had gotten that poem from, I decided not to mention it. I knew that they had been inspired by her husband. As I remember, he was the author of "Inspiration".

She softly chuckled. "He had told me of his plans. I couldn't have agreed with him more—he felt you deserved it, and he couldn't have given it to a nicer gentleman."

"Your compliment is appreciated, ma'am."

"Very deserving. And regarding our friend PeggyAnn, I'm glad that she gave those clippings to you. You will always have those, as well, to remember them by. Photos say a thousand words."

"Can never be replaced," I agreed with her one hundred percent. When I glanced toward the area where all her pictures were nicely arranged, I also noticed, on one wall, a very familiar piece of art. At least, it appeared to be what I had assumed. Since I couldn't get a good look at it from where I sat, my eyes could have easily deceived me because of the angle. It faced the opposite wall. Curiosity knocked. I asked before picking up a fresh glass of iced-cold lemonade, "Is that some of your artwork hanging on the far wall?"

Dr. Johnston turned toward the direction I was looking in. She stood up with the pictures in her hand. "You're referring to the drawing of Josephine and me." She walked toward the shelf. "You're welcome to my little gallery over here," she invited me, smiling, proud of her prized possessions.

I got up, too, and followed her.

Further giving me an introduction of the display, she added, "This area is where I visit from, time to time, to reflect on special moments." She set the frames back on the shelves then gazed over the population of snapshots. They were obviously her treasure, a rainbow of crops exhibiting some serious and smiling faces.

"As you have said, 'Photos say a thousand words.' And these certainly cannot be replaced. These are years of memories."

As eye-catching as they were, what drew my initial attention took me elsewhere. Finally facing the two girls in

the drawing on the wall, I sailed beyond their shadows...
At last, the finale plays, softly, deep beyond the walls and crevices of my eyes. Like the finest of art, the sax got the best of my imagination. I had been lured again by the power of its musical attraction. It drew me further into the distance. There they were—both Genesis and Josephine, staring out the window as before. Mesmerized. Their escape had a certain drawing power. Fascinating. Just as before, I heard nothing but smoothly suave music of a past, draping like fallen snow. The charming and warm image suddenly disappeared.

"This is special," Dr. Johnston said straight from the heart. She gazed at the drawing with great pride. "Originally, PeggyAnn had drawn this back home when I was only ten-years-old. Later, her daughter, Idella, redrew it in color and drafted it in a larger size. I'll show you the original." She turned and picked up a large photo album. When opened, the original sketch laid neatly inside.

I examined the smaller version, then looked at the larger one on the wall. "That's amazing. They are identical."

"Aren't they?" she agreed. "Fantastic work." She ran her finger across PeggyAnn's smooth signature.

We both stood there, admiring the art in our own way. One—a beautiful and, once, withdrawn young girl. The other...was only a witness. It symbolized something so real to her, and it had true meaning for me. Being at the scene interlocked each of our destinies in the most unusual way.

I smiled at the lovely drawing, thinking, *So, that's what Ms. PeggyAnn drew in the Bailey's home. She's good.* The art revealed no signs of Genesis being unhappy. They were so calm and peaceful. Somewhere serene. I guessed that was the way Ms. PeggyAnn wanted it to be. End on a happy note. It looked so real, as if it were yesterday.

Since they were good friends, I commented, "It had to be difficult when all of you had to go your separate ways. That must've been tough." I turned toward the other pictures, scoping the crops of photos, again.

Dr. Johnston closed the photo album and put it away. "Yes, it was. We all left Oklahoma for different reasons." She joined me where I stood and reached for a specific picture. "This photo was taken when Joshua and I married." She passed it to me.

I grinned, wondering, if the snapshot was taken at the same church as in the dream. "In Earlsboro?" I had to ask. If so, some external updates had been made. Back in the day, it looked plain and lonely. Nothing about the area, in general, would've drawn much attention, but, surprisingly, the photo exposed some stimulating upgrades. Some shrubbery and other added details complimented the landscape and made the black and white photo just that much more appealing.

She seemed utterly surprised.

I wanted to laugh but decided not to. Rather, I added, "In Earlsboro...with one ear?" My eyes were like beams, gazing at her, wanting to burst into tears.

Uncontrollably, she laughed. "Umph, umph, umph. I haven't heard that before."

Stuck, she couldn't get past Earlsboro having one ear. Neither could I. And more so, the thought reminded me of spurs and boots, soaring mountains, and a cactus. Somewhere...very far from civilization.

She went on to say, "Earlsboro...with one ear." Her head twitched. "I have to remember that." Her eyes were watery.

I saw a tissue box nearby and handed it to her. She pulled out a sheet. Raising her glasses, she swept away the flood that streamed down her face.

"I didn't mean to make you cry," I chuckled.

At that moment, she didn't seem to really know what to say. She only shook her head and was probably wondering where we had left off before my timely comment.

Getting her back on track, I helped her out. "Maybe, I should rephrase that question. Did you get married in Earlsboro, Oklahoma?"

While trying to compose herself, she answered, "Yes, we did." When it registered, she looked up and, puzzled, asked, "You knew?"

I was enjoying the conversation with Dr. Johnston to the point that I said a little more than I should have. As a quick fix, I patched her curiosity and told her with a smile, "It's just a wild guess. Earlsboro seems to be the most likely place."

Her forehead rose as she nodded in utmost agreement, "Yes, I could see that. Your wild guess is right. However, we all didn't say vows in one place. I miss those days when we all were together in the country. PeggyAnn was the nucleus of our circle. She had a heart of gold. So did the man she married."

Deep inside my memory bank, I couldn't pull up a flash card on him. It dawned on me that, during my fireside chat with Ms. PeggyAnn, she had never gone that far into detail. I had not thought to ask. "He had to be for Ms. PeggyAnn to take a liking to him." I gave her the wedding photo back.

She scanned it once more before placing it back on the shelf. "Leathie Velt was an extremely kind man. When they left for the West, they moved a long way from home."

I agreed, "Many miles in-between. That is a number of states away."

"They were musically put together."

Musically put together? I asked myself. *What does that mean?* Baffled by the unusual statement, she had my undivided attention. Eager to get more information, I inquired, "How so?" Knowing that area well, I had to find out what she meant.

"She knew music, and so did Leathie. From what I understood, he went from guitar to piano to singing without batting an eye." Animation soared through her voice. "Lawd knows what else he did!"

Drifting, once more, Ms. PeggyAnn came into view... *I saw her beautiful, smiling face and heard her laughing while she unraveled fascinating moments of reflections in my tea. Intrigued by the new revelation, it didn't take long to filter. I wasn't surprised, remembering the white flag. Her handkerchief followed her wherever she went. A few seconds later, the shadow vanished. And soon, so did the remnants of the final rendition, as it skipped along the musical scale and pivoted into a leaning whisper. Its mist trailed as lightly as feathers, as Dr. Johnston's voice merged.*

"...And that goes for his entire family, including the down line."

I became weak from watching this lady shift into another mode. Since I had been in deep thought, I wondered what else she might have said. I chuckled and thought, *Umph. That's funny.* Her eyes seemed as though they had bulged clearly above her spectacles. *Musically put together—I've never heard of that.*

"Well put," I told her.

"Dear...it's the truth and nothing but the truth!"

I joined in the moment of her reflections of the two and added, stepping back, "And Truth set them free." My next thought came to a screeching halt. I hadn't realized that the music had stopped.

We were staring silence in the face. Out of nowhere, startled, I heard what sounded like my personal pianist. The volume level pierced through the entire room with richness, eloquence, and expression.

Dr. Johnston read my mind. "Does that sound familiar?" she knowingly smiled.

"It does," I nodded. Listening, dazed, my pulse started EKG'n to the beat. Impeccable creativity was masterfully on display in the slow, peppy speed. *That is Freddie the Teddy.*

His name raced across my mind. I slightly grinned. "I could recognize my pianist anywhere." No other musician played, at the moment, but him.

"Camille gave Marcella a copy of your most recent CD before she left. I'm glad she brought it by. He's good."

"One of the greatest I've ever come in contact with."

"Well," she said, turning the other way, "I'm ready to return to my chair and listen to more of his spectacular delivery."

I glanced at my watch. "I'll join you." Then, something very compelling occurred to me. Time was on my side. I retrieved my glass of lemonade and drank a couple swallows. Much of the ice had melted, but, to my delight, the chill awakened my dry throat.

Dr. Johnston stated, "I'm thirsty, too. I've laughed so much…"

Remembering Mr. Bailey's request could not have come too soon. Now…I had to fulfill a promise I had made. Timing couldn't have been better.

She sat in her chair. Before she finished her drink, I had already put mine down.

"Does this sound familiar?" I redirected her previous question, catching her totally off guard. "For you…Nan Mother."

The machinery of my head and extremities were mechanically in operation. At the perfect moment, I blended in with Freddie as I listened to each profound note that dribbled through his magical fingers. He had set the tone for me to drift to whichever place I chose to go, which, in any climate, I was ready to roll.

Right on time, I had stolen her immediate attention. When she realized what was taking place, she sat back, comfortably beaming.

"Oh, Lawd," I heard her say, "this is getting better and better." She shook her head in disbelief, seemingly dazed.

If I had looked at her any longer, it would have been nearly impossible to finish. That, of course, was hard to do.

Before I knew it, Josie had rushed in and sat on the sofa with the sweetest smile. Engaged, her head motioned. Marcella came in behind her and stood beside Dr. Johnston. Amazement highlighted her face.

My arms swayed in sync with the rhythm of my assembly. In stride with the current of beats, I took on the high plains and vocalized the lower ones. Which seasoning I vocally applied depended on the climate of what I felt. It was never in the forecast. However, before this mission ended, I dashed and whipped through the last drizzle of raining music. The weather condition, musically, was one I had to archive because Freddie's musical plea brought out the thunder and the rain.

I just listened in rhythm to the flow of his ongoing music. He had a style that was all his own, capable of dismantling any conversation in air, on land, or sea. I had once heard, in an audience, a woman say, in good humor, "Who better to calm Mother Nature's disruptions? Being that good, Mother Nature would have changed her mind and sat down, herself, to listen and cool off. If severe weather tried to approach on that man's territory, while in progress, she would reprimand and suspend her own party—INDEFINITELY." Silently, I chuckled at something Freddie had once said, "If there's to be any severe weather taking place, it would happen from the ambers of our own private world." Freddie loved his style of great sunshiny weather, but he would always say, too, "I know it won't always be sunny, Devin, but whatever else you want to do—drizzle, rain, or thunder—just sing white as snow." We both had gotten a laugh or two from that statement, then went for it. And, just as if we were together, live today, I gave it my all.

...WHEW! When it rains, it pours...

GLISSANDO!

Glissando is a technique,
an artistic sound,
harmonic physique;
a skill,
style,
stories to tell,
rapidly sliding,
up or down the musical scale.

Its timing is critical,
waiting to leap,
murmuring while steeping,
in the suspense,
while footprints whisper,
in-between lines of their sheet music,
rhyming with the times,
unfurling echoes…
REWIND!

Reminiscing,
what history wrote,
deploying scenes,
stunning notes,
on time,
in sync,
critiqued,
GLISSANDO…
complete.

…its calligraphy is painted by smooth rhythm and style.

Chapter 17

DEVIN

I walked along the streets of Atlantic Station, dazed, as warm air made its presence known all around me before being swept away by an unexpected current. On the street, vehicles crept or were at a standstill. They moved along the busy two-way street and, eventually, faded from view as crowds flashed by. Similarly, my mind had taken on this same pattern of movement. My psyche had been occupied and teased as if thoughts cruised, paused, and rolled, freely, gliding in transit. From the moment I left Nan Mother's home, I revisited memorable scenes from the very beginning. And, during the process, I couldn't seem to stop smiling within. Never had it crossed my mind that there would be a continuation. Deep inside the cove in my head was where the beacon of this particular story flashed on the meadow. It started as a dream and nothing but a dream until I met some very special but key people. First, it was Ms. PeggyAnn, who turned out to be the catalyst. She had ignited its creation. Then, there was Joshua and Josephine, and, finally, Genesis…plus a whole new cast. Amazing. Never would I have thought I would actually meet the characters that had lived in my imagination. *And I guess this is where the chapter ends*, a little voice said. As significant as it was, this legendary encounter would always be a special part of my life. Putting the reflection on hold, I focused more on the direction I was heading in.

In front of well-known and exquisite shops, vehicles were lined along both sides of the road. The shopping strip on multiple streets drew in plenty of curiosity from around every corner. Smells of food had their drawing power, too, and spectators took advantage of it.

As I crossed the way, my timing could not have been better as I saw all three of my family members getting out of a pearl-white SUV. *Pops didn't drive after all.* Apparently, his plans had changed.

A little ways away, I picked up a little speed, just enough to get to them hopefully before they vanished. Even so, we had already decided where to meet.

Very much needed, this was the nearest, best thing to exercise I had gotten all day. My adrenaline was on the rise, percolating. My thoughts had done plenty for most of the day because of all the unexpected occurrences. Now, my lower extremities were in stride, incurring just what they lacked and needed during my time away from home. Chopping through gravity, I reached them quickly.

Pop turned and smiled. "Here he is…" he patted me on the shoulder.

"It's me!" I grinned. "How is everyone doing?"

"Fine," they chorused.

"Good timing," Pop said.

I glanced at my watch. "Not bad. With all that has transpired within the last few hours, I've done well."

With a hint of concern in her voice, Mom asked, "Is everything all right?" She stood in-between the others, who, now, were all curious.

"It certainly is." I couldn't bear to hold it in. Some disbelief had mixed in my response.

Imani's eyes dazzled. "Sounds like you've had quite a morning," she commented.

My eyes grew slightly. "Interesting and well spent. I'll never forget it. That's for sure. There's only one word to describe it."

"You have my undivided attention," were Pop's exact words. He didn't move nor bat an eye.

"Fascinating… One of the most gripping I've ever experienced."

Pop smiled. "Are you getting married?"

Realizing how I must've sounded, I smoothly laughed and replied, "Sorry for the disappointment but that's a 'no' to your question."

"Well…it was a good thought," he said, realizing he had tried but failed. "Fascinating. Gripping. Whatever it is, I'm anxious to hear about it."

"I must fill you in."

Imani edged in, "Devin, it's nothing like that—"

I smoothly chuckled before she could finish. "No, thank goodness." I knew exactly what had entered her mind. Since the other two had no clue what Imani was referring to, I chipped away at their curiosity, "It's nothing that you don't already know about."

They smiled, still, with wonder in their eyes.

Releasing that thought, I added and emphasized, "But this"—I paused—"I have to tell you what happened earlier. And what I have to say is too deep to explain in a few words."

Pop nodded, "All right. Hold that thought." Then, he decided to say, "It's time to get a little something to eat. Ready for brunch?" He gazed at the women. "I already know about Devin. We stick together," he joked, in the mood to entertain a little. "Like father, like son. If he's still anything like me, he doesn't miss a meal."

"Ready, if you are," I grinned.

Both women seemed to have coordinated their familiar response as a team, "We always stick together—like mom, like daughter. We're ready, also."

"Beautiful, I'm sticking with you, too," Pop declared charmingly to Mom.

We laughed, sealing the plan unanimously.

He glanced in both directions, then walked toward the door of the eatery and told me, "You can tell us about it inside. Let's head for a table."

As we entered the building, his cell phone rang.

Being a grown man, my story telling days weren't over yet. While I comfortably sat at a table, I filled them in on my visit at Dr. Johnston's home. Their various expressions didn't go by unnoticed, but I had to remain focused. During the process, my emotions inclined multiple times, reflecting on the chain of events. If they only knew the depth of what I had experienced, that would have given them an even clearer picture of why it was fascinating and gripping. There were too many missing links, and, eventually, they would have to envision it through my eyes to understand the significance. I knew, by the time I finished, there would be an onset of questions. And just as I had suspected, an imprint formed between Pop's eyes as curiosity leaped from off the page of his face. It left a mark of pure astonishment.

"You had never met this lady before?"

Beyond shocked, I verified, "No…but yes."

"That's an interesting reply, Devin," Mom stated.

My answer was, "It goes much deeper than what I have already shared." I looked down at the table as I managed to cough up a chuckle. What I had experienced, I knew the three would be just as amazed, but, at the same time, would find something of this magnitude a little hard to believe.

"I have a feeling…whatever it is," Imani stressed jokingly, "it will not be the norm."

"Sis, if you only knew."

Each of them sat up straight, listening, opting to open the floor for me to elaborate. The anticipation showed in their body language.

Knowing I didn't have time to go into great detail about the dream, I, instead, decided to share with them only enough information to get a clear picture. I felt as though I didn't know where to start. So much information was beginning to block the door of my thought process. After taking a deep breath, I sat back and relaxed. Because I didn't want to prolong what I had to say any further, I said, "Let me explain and start from the very beginning. Interestingly, this dream takes place in…"

Just as I began my introduction, I looked up and saw that everyone's expressions had changed. The spell had been broken. A man suddenly approached our table.

My water almost tipped over, but I caught it just in time. The remarkable story I was prepared to reflect on, which they had waited so patiently to hear about, skidded.

As if things couldn't get any stranger, there he stood— the same man I had seen at the park. *He looks…just…like…* That thought staggered. The way I felt, I needed speech therapy. I couldn't believe it.

Pop smiled, "Here's Paul. Have a seat."

"I hope I didn't take too long," the man said.

Completely stunned, I stared in disbelief, while looking straight through the guy.

"Devin," Pop energetically said, snapping me back to reality, "here's the cousin I wanted you to meet. Haven't seen him since the Civil War." He cackled. That gave me an idea about just how long it had been. Many years ago. Maybe, even, before my time.

Paul laughed, "Now...that is a long time ago. Wasn't President Lincoln in office then?"

They were casual in their conversation, which let me know that they had shared some memorable times together back in the day.

On the same note, I shared some, too, gazing at a splitting image that had settled deep in my memory bank. I couldn't help noticing the distinguished patch of gray hair that stood out, shining, on the corner of his head. Lowly, I mumbled, "That's impossible." The similarities sent me reeling into instant shock.

Pop admitted, "Well, I may have exaggerated a little."

"You're still Lance, and I wouldn't have it any other way," his cousin replied, then looked my way.

Smiling at a stark realization, I gladly extended my arm, "Awesome to meet you, Paul."

"Hey, Devin, it's my honor," he grinned and shook my hand with a power grip. A beacon of kindness was lodged behind his eyes.

"Likewise. In more ways than one."

That statement seemed to have come across as striking to everyone else.

The waitress came. "Is everyone ready?"

I let Pop have the honor of responding since company had just arrived. He replied, "Give us about five more minutes. That will give our guest some time to look over the menu."

Paul immediately said, "We can proceed now if everyone else is ready. I know what I would like to have. I'm no stranger here."

She took our orders then left to serve the other customers.

Still focused on where we had left off, I looked directly at Pop as I continued the conversation, "*This is your cousin?*" That was one question I couldn't forget, no matter how long it took for the waitress to complete our orders. I wanted him to reconfirm what I thought might have been a mistake, even though Paul's features and physique were not figments of my imagination. Since he didn't have on the hat and dark sunglasses that he had worn the other day, I now saw even more etchings of his face.

With a proud reply, he answered, "Yes, he is."

"Not too many people I know have that name. As a matter-of-fact, I only know of two. Your name is rather interesting, from my standpoint," I told Paul.

"Is it?" he said, engaged. "How so?"

"Well," I chuckled, "it's a long story, but I will say this. In short, one of them that I am familiar with is a triplet. The man was famous during his time."

Paul immediately gazed at Pop. He appeared intrigued.

I continued, "I met him. He and his—"

"Devin, what year are you from?"

Everyone laughed.

"Paul," I chuckled, briefly reflecting on some history that I knew he wouldn't be able to relate to as I had, "I'm a twenty-first century type of guy."

"Good answer! I have to remember that one."

Oddly, Mom and Pop glanced at one another. I wondered what had run across their minds.

Paul refrained from asking any further questions, and I couldn't blame him.

Imani's countenance of curiosity seeped through. "You're a twenty-first century type of guy, aaaand" she tried to match up what didn't sound quite right to her, "you know all three triplets back—" She looked baffled.

I had to laugh. Her expression ran deep.

"That's stranger than anything I have ever heard you say," those words spooled from her mouth.

"If the shoe was reversed, I probably would have said the same thing. That's part of what I wanted to share with all of you earlier."

"In connection with what happened to you at the lady's home this morning?" Pop edged in to say.

"Yes. It's deep."

"I have to hear this. You met them..." His words seemed to have gotten stuck in mid-air. "That's something I need a clearer understanding on."

The rest of them agreed, including Paul.

Ironically, my eyes landed on Mom's finger. I spotted the shiny diamond and symbol that reminded me of the story's significance and roots. As I retold the chain of events, I relived special moments just as they happened in consecutive order but, in a much shorter version. Otherwise, it would have taken hours. I felt piercing eyes staring from every direction. By the time I had gotten around to meeting Mr. Jackson and his brothers, Pop mysteriously intervened.

"That is quite interesting and, foremost, ironic."

When I saw Paul's expression, he appeared a little shocked, himself. Not surprised, I knew he had plenty of questions to ask from where that came from.

"In what way," I asked, wanting to get back to my visitation rights.

"Devin, this dream of yours...is so real. I can envision it just as you are telling it. The triplets...umph," Pop said with amazement spiraling in his voice and shaking his head the whole while. A grin was trying to break through the features of his face but the dynamics of what I had revealed were still filtering. "Humph," he then looked at Mom and asked, "Can you believe this?"

"Honestly, no, Lance."

Lost, I asked him, "What is it, Pop?"

Imani glanced at me. She nodded and smiled then shook her head.

I was confused by her mixed reactions.

Pop continued, "There is something your mother and I need to tell you."

Because of their expressions, they had my undivided attention.

"Not so many days ago," he went on, "your Grandfather Lester had me to stop by before we left Greensboro, North Carolina to pick up a couple items for you. Instead of bringing them along, we sent them via Fed-Ex to your home before we left, so it would be there by the time you arrived back in California. No sense in you lugging those around; you would've winded up shipping them anyway. He shared with us what his mother, Leen-Onme, had told him."

Abruptly, out of curiosity, I said, "Leen-Onme. Not to change the subject but, *where did she get that name?*"

He replied in a voice a little higher than normal, "Devin, I have *no* idea. All I know is that…she was greatly admired in the community, as well as in her church. I remember her from long ago. A good lady. The neighborhood children and I were crazy about her."

I nodded for him to proceed, listening intently.

"Well, Lester informed us that the items had twinkled down from her grandfather but had no real home. From what I understood, they had been boxed up since my great-great-grandfathers left them behind. I say all that to say this—your great-great-great-grandfathers…*were the triplets.*"

"What!" I almost jumped out of my skin. "Moses! David! And Paul!!!"

"It is true," my mother smiled. "I heard it with my very own ears. That is rather remarkable."

Paul gave his affirmation, "I had heard a little about them some time ago. Ironically, that's where my name derived from. At least, that's what I've been told."

My reply was, "You were given the right name because, in the dream, you are a splitting image of him. That's why

I went into shock when you approached our table. I can't believe it," I shook my head in disbelief. At the same time, I was honored and delighted that Mr. Jackson and the others were a part of the family.

Pop added, "I was just talking to Paul about it at the park the other day. Papa Lester didn't know much about them, but he knows some things, but he said that his mother also said something else that comes as a surprise, now that I think about it." He looked at Mom, "Remember, ReJoyce, when Lester stated that my grandmother had said that the tale had been that Paul told a relative that he had had a strange dream? And you're not going to believe this either."

"What's that?" I embraced myself.

"He said a unique person appeared in his dream. And, ironically, his name…was Devin."

Speechless, I couldn't say a word.

Everyone had been taken by the news and were just as mum until I wondered who would speak next.

"Wow," Imani responded first, "that's unbelievable."

Mom commented, "Sounds like that tale had some truth to it."

Remembering something that had seemed like nonsense earlier, I spontaneously asked Paul, mesmerized, "Are you a triplet, man!"

Everybody around the table laughed, including me.

My eyes went on the hunt. "Yeah, Paul, I don't know." At that point, it wasn't an unlikely question, considering what I now knew. It was a thought just in case two more unexpected replicas walked inside the building.

"Only me," he replied with comedy in his voice. He had cackled to the point that his eyes were watery, flooding overboard.

"Umph," I then said, "I had to ask."

"I see your point," he flagged his hand, letting me know that there were no other look alikes. "Only one sister. You have nothing to worry about."

Getting back to the topic, I said, "I have to thank Grandpop Lester for the items."

"He'll love that. And he also said," Pop continued, "he had forgotten that he'd had them safely put away. His mind was triggered when he saw a photo, which reminded him of the tale. He stated that his mother always thought that you were the one who should have them."

Imani said, impressed, peering at me, "That is so interesting. I'm curious to hear what happened next."

From a combination of bewilderment, shock, surprises and laughter, her last statement kept right on scrolling. I had a delayed reaction. "Next?" Suddenly, I remembered. "Oh, yeah. The dream."

"Is there more?" Pop asked.

"Yes, there is."

Just in time to refresh my mind and regroup, the waitress returned and served our meals.

"Thank you," we chorused.

"My pleasure."

After they had finished the light meal, they were ready and interested in hearing the continuation. I drank a few swallows of juice rather than my usual smooth tea. I played it safe since my storytelling antidote seemed to take me, at times, on extended trips far beyond my imagination. Light years into the galaxy of my mind, the dream had been a prime example. In a place I had never even heard of, I wound up waaaaaay in Seminole County. And even more interesting, I didn't know, during the excursion, how long the layover would last. Although appalled, it turned out to be one of the best trips ever. And, I didn't regret it. However, this time, I wouldn't be in an altered state, I would only be giving a recap—nice, short, and sweet.

I took one last swallow for the countdown as chatter at our table came to a hush. Refreshed, I remembered exactly where I had left off... *Drifting into solitude as if I was really there, I could still hear that same sax raining from earlier today. So much class was softly pacing in my crib from deep within. My thoughts swayed in its gravity, note by note, as I proceeded, "And the beat goes on like this..."*

The music in my head stopped when Mom cut in, "Who is Grandfather Clock?"

From the expression on her face, I couldn't decipher if she was confused or shocked.

"All I know is the man's name is Mr. Alexander, and he had been labeled Grandfather Clock because he was the pendulum of music and chimed right on time. From what I've heard, he had been rated as unusually and awesomely dynamic. Better put, he was magnificent."

"Heard? Heard from whom?"

Her line of questioning struck me as odd. I wondered where this was going. My antenna went up, quickly, as I answered, "Ms. PeggyAnn."

"Are you speaking of the lady in the dream?"

"Well...yes," I paused. "She is real."

Pop, then, intervened. "She is?" Traces of bewilderment lodged in his eyes.

Grinning, I replied, "Yes. Absolutely."

"Did you hear that, ReJoyce?" he gazed at her. "That's an amazing story."

"I haven't gotten to that part yet, but I'll fill you in about her, too."

Mom smiled, "Your story is so intriguing. Quite frankly, it's...a jaw dropper. There's a reason why I asked about this person Grandfather Clock. Do you know his complete name?" I noticed she was turning one of her rings round and round, listening intently.

"Never found that out. The man came and went like a ghost."

She reached for her purse, pulled out a photo, and handed it to me. "Is this him?"

As soon as I surveyed the antiquated, black-and-white picture, I visualized the man who had walked into Ruby's restaurant. A case of mistaken identity was impossible. I recognized him and said, dazed, "Yes, that's him. Do you know this guy?" My eyes inquisitively traveled in her direction. Intensity grew by the second. It was equivalent to a phenomenon on the brink, waiting to happen. Just as they, I had been captured.

Shedding more light on the subject, she let me know, "No, I do not know him, but I know who he is. His name is John Zachariah Alexander. He has quite an impressive name." She smiled now that the mystery had been cracked.

Imani and Paul exchanged words.

Glancing at the icon, once more, my head twitched. Glad to know a little more history on this individual, I nodded my head, agreeing with her, "That fits him." But one other thing zipped to the forefront of my brain, radiating, *How does she know his name?*

That thought must've been transparent because she immediately proceeded, saying, "There's more."

Pop emphatically cut in. "There sure is. I'm surprised we didn't know about him long before now."

A burning question leaped, "Who is he...really?"

The suspense burst when she added, "He's known as 'GFC,' which stands for 'Grandfather Clock.' He's a very important man. I don't know of any other words that best describe the news other than what you have used earlier. Talk about fascinating and gripping—he is my great-grandfather, your...great-great-grandfather."

My legs sprang like jumping beans as I stood up out of my chair. "ReJoyce!" I exclaimed with some exhilaration and extreme shock. A glissando spiraled through my nervous system because of the surprising news. Unexpectedly, I had drawn a little attention to myself from several neighboring customers.

"That's right!" one of them said.

Then, an elderly lady chimed in, "It is written to rejoice." Her eyes were wide behind the rim of her glasses.

I smiled, "Yes, it is." She, among others, stole my attention. Her animation and charm had a striking effect. Taken by her character, she reminded me of others that I had had the opportunity of coming in contact with. I saw similarities but, just like fingerprints are different, she had her own unique way about herself.

The man that accompanied her turned and smiled. He nodded, "Amen to that."

Embarrassed by my spontaneous outburst, I wondered how I was going to offset the situation. Realizing that the queen of my family, herself, had such a unique name, all I could do, for the moment, was chuckle. I didn't know what had gotten into me, but, evidently, my response had sent a good message. *Umph.* One powerful word leaped off the bench of my mouth and stirred witnesses.

Everyone at my table had laughed, almost into hysterics.

"That appears to be 'what you do best,' Devin," were Pop's words to encourage. "You are a man of inspiration. There's nothing wrong with utilizing it."

A man walked up. "You're the artist, aren't you?"

"Which one? Since I have drawn a clear picture of myself."

The guy appeared baffled by the statement but joined in the spirit of laughter, anyway.

"To answer your question, yes, I am Devin Fairchild."

"I'm the manager," he reached out his hand. "Nice to meet you."

I sealed the handshake. "Likewise."

He glanced at everyone around the table, acknowledging them. "I want to thank you for stopping by. We would love for you and your family to come back anytime."

"Thank you. It won't be my last visit."

He beamed. "Good." Elation rang in his voice. "I don't know what prompted all the excitement over here, but it got my attention loudly and clearly. Drawn to share the news and, because of you, I have made a very important decision. I have been trying to figure it out for the longest, but now I know."

I smiled at the guy who appeared relieved. "What decision would that be?" my curiosity burned.

"Our newborn doesn't have a name yet, so, I have decided to call her Rejoice. Has a nice ring. Besides, it has meaning. Thank you."

After that, I no longer had any reason to feel as though I needed to rectify my actions. It was already done.

Bubbling over inside, I nodded. "You're welcome. When I return, I look forward to seeing a picture of the little one. Hopefully, you'll still be working here. If not, maybe, our paths will cross again."

"I'm all for that, and…rejoice on. I know I will." He acknowledged the others. Then, he left.

Compelling…there it was again. The rendition hit the rooftop, dancing in my head in a spiraling fashion of music. *Wow*, I thought as I sat back down in my chair, engaged in its harmonic physique and the chatter that surrounded me. Its artistic sound flushed right on through with skill and style as if it thundered to exhale. It had a story to tell of its own. Rapidly sliding up and down the musical scale of the baby grand, the rendition was timely, and its timing could not have been better as we reminisced on what history had written. As critical as it was to be on point, the explosion waited to leap, murmuring, while steeping in the suspense of the unknown. Those who had affected our lives were footprints whispered from imprints in-between lines of their sheet music. And today, the footprints of each character echoed as each revelation unfurled. Their destinies chimed, rhyming with the times.

In addition, knowing who Moses, David, Paul, and GFC really were, there was a reason why I had to rewind the scenes and let the music play. The glissando was unique as scenes deployed each individual's stunning note. It struck, rising from the cavity of my mind on time and in sync—critiqued. Now, it was complete, but it didn't stop there. The sax had long vanished and ended its finale. So, I thought. It blended right in the orchestration. After days of trying to crack wide-open the string of mysteries, I could now hear the creativity of all the other apparatuses that chimed in. Each that had been teasing my mental faculty had finally touched down in full rhythm. I understood their precision, in toto. At last, the mysteries had unfolded.

…Wow, the beat was spellbinding…

PAUSE

Chapter 18

DEVIN

My plane landed in Los Angeles. Shifting in thought, rotational faces and scenes appeared of what had transpired over the past few days then quickly faded as I also watched activities that took place at the airport. From my window seat in first class, I watched the nighttime arrivals and departures. They were just as interesting to observe as during the daytime hours. Aircrafts were scrolling by in fast and in slow motion. The view was amazing, as if I had been watching it all live on an enormous screen. The huge mechanical birds taxied the runways consecutively and orderly. Whether arriving or departing, they seemingly were on a mission, especially aircrafts that were preparing for takeoff. As if to salute the nation, their escapes sounded off, leaving a trail of good-byes across the skyline as it disappeared into the night.

Walking out the terminal, vehicles and transporters were barely moving. Although many travelers were returning or leaving because of the holiday weekend, the airport had become a parking lot. More so busier than the norm, a traffic jam was not unusual. After navigating through the congestion, I dashed into the parking deck. Like the airplanes, I, too, vanished into the night.

Now, since the mysteries, during my trip, had shut their eyes, they had chanted into silence. The next day, as I walked into my kitchen, I slightly smiled, thinking, *The purple melody has ended. Or has it?* Then, I wondered, *Could there possibly be other mysteries waiting to whisper and cast spells on my imagination? If so, whose and what other melody could possibly fall splendidly like rain as before?* That very thought made me wonder just how true that could be. I listened. With no problem, I could musically replay history since clarity of those mysteries were now clear. Amazing how the rendition intertwined into a nice contrast of those involved. They were channeled into view in high definition and resolution. What made it so special was that they had been specifically and melodically inscribed with history. I just let it play and drift above the planes of my imagination, where notes descriptively rang about special people. Most importantly, the genetics of right changed the genetics of their worlds. That was why their melodies beautifully glowed in the purple dawn. And it couldn't get any better than that. Eyes of my imagination were set, eloquently threading the royalty of purple through their striking melodies. The amazing site of tunes was stunningly in full bloom. I had injected gold into the music because extracts of their lives had spoken for themselves. Maybe, someday, the purple melody would snow again. If more was to come, it had paused for now.

Although the rendition may have halted, some things, on the other hand, just couldn't be placed on hold. Inevitably, I remained in a daze, trying to filter the latest headlines. My life had been unbelievably affected. It never ceased to amaze me how everything unraveled and hit home. Meeting Paul was just another reminder that everyone had a twin out there somewhere, but his twin wasn't just anyone. He resembled Mr. Jackson so much until I thought for a minute that I had relapsed into the past and couldn't come out of it. *Mr. Jackson is actually a relative.* Since coming into the knowledge of that discovery, I didn't know how many times that had skipped in my head. Not only were we kin, but he was my great-great-great grandfather. "HA-HAAAAAA," I laughed out, humored by the thought as I walked out of the kitchen with a glass of water in my hand.

When I thought of Moses and David, I laughed again. Even so, I couldn't be more appreciative of knowing that they were kinfolk who I would treasure for life. In the same breath, I would have never thought that Grandfather Clock and I were related. "Shocked" was an understatement. It most likely would take a while before it all finally sunk in; however, it was all good. Even better, it was great news.

I stood in front of the sliding door and observed the perimeter as I drank a few swallows of water. The only thing I'd heard since being back in town, so far, had been the phone and the television. Jordache had not occupied her space since I'd been gone. Without her around and patrolling the backyard, it was noticeable. Soon, she would be home to fill her spot. Then, everything would be back to normal.

Not more than ten seconds later, I heard a big truck. It suddenly came to a squeaky halt. I drank the rest of the water and returned to the kitchen to set the glass on the counter. When I saw the Fed-Ex truck, I remembered the box I had shipped. It couldn't be in better hands since the box that Nan Mother had given me had the word FRAGILE stamped on it. It needed to be handled with care.

When the deliveryman came to the door, he greeted me, "Mr. Fairchild, how are you doing today?" I was no stranger since he had delivered to my residence on more than a few occasions.

"I'm doing well, and yourself?"

"Doing good."

"I'll take that," I told him, taking the not-so-light box out of his tight grip. Made me wonder what was inside. Its weight put pressure on the muscles.

He chuckled. "I also have five more items for you. I'll be right back."

When I saw that the items were practically the same in height and width, except two, I met him at the path to help until all six were accounted for.

"Whew," I said, signing my John Hancock, "I'm glad I was here to receive them. I had no idea this many boxes were coming. If I had to pick those up from Fed-Ex, I would have worked up a little sweat."

The guy chuckled. "I know what you mean. The day is not over for me. I still have more to deliver, but, after a while, you get used to it."

"One thing is for sure—it's good exercise."

"Yes, it is." After he took what he needed, he was ready to move along.

"Thank you, and have a gymnasium day."

"I will," he cackled, and so did I.

As I shut the door, I turned and scanned each item in the middle of the floor. I immediately recognized the box I had shipped. Before I pried into any of the others, I reached for that particular one and walked to the dining area and set it on top of the table. When I opened it, the item inside had been secured with bubble wrap and a layer of protective foam was around it. Once I undraped it, my mouth gaped. There sat Joshua's saxophone inside a showcase. I stood back, admiring the apparatus, then said lowly, "I can't believe it." In disbelief, I picked it up. Before I sat it back down, I felt something on the bottom of the base. When I looked underneath, I saw that a key, wrapped inside plastic, had been securely attached. I detached it and searched for an obvious keyhole. After locating it, I unlocked it and figured out how to get the sax out. I held the shiny, historical masterpiece proudly in my hands. Taken by pure astonishment, I could only say, "Un…believable." Observing it, I noticed plastic inside of the mouth of the horn, but, before I could further entertain getting it out, something else grabbed my immediate attention. In the most impressive artwork, I was shocked to see GOLDIE engraved in its pure skin. It had been etched multiple times in a circle. "Is this you, Goldie?" I said out loud as if the icon could talk back. Fortunately, no one was around to hear. Next, the obvious leaped from my mind. "Mr. Jackson!" I chuckled as I turned and scoped out my home like a P.I., as if someone really could have heard me. Releasing that humorous thought, I turned the horn over. The plastic fell out onto the table. Inside were new reeds for the mouthpiece. I smiled, then dropped them back inside the opening. Immediately, I went into another room and got a piece of soft cloth. Before placing Goldie back in position, I polished her pure skin, erasing my fingerprints. Afterward, I locked her inside, then decided to put all the wrapping contents into the box. As I was about to drop those items inside, I saw something laying at the bottom. I reached for the white envelope. I opened it and read:

Dear Devin,

How could I ever forget the evening we first met? Some people, places, and things are never forgotten. And you are one of those individuals who will long be remembered. On that "cherishable" note, this is not a long letter but just a brief enclosure to let you know that the saxophone packaged inside has been one of my memorable joys. A very dear friend of mine, Paul Jackson, passed it on to me many years ago. As a matter-of-fact, it was decades ago. Although I never played it, it has been a delight to observe and an honor to behold.

Having the pleasure of meeting you and having the opportunity to watch you perform, on more than one occasion, has left a great impression on me. Josephine and I have performed many days ourselves. In doing so, we were graciously blessed along the way. It has been one of our tokens of love toward humanity. From what I saw and heard, you are one of the greatest. If Paul only knew, he would agree. My final words are…this belongs to you. The torch is now in your hands.

Joy and peace toward all,

Joshua Johnston
"Inspire"

Strangely, I had not realized that I had sat down. Moved, I read it again and again. Captivated by the contents, it seemed as though I had read it without blinking. My eyes scrolled above the rim of the paper. My binoculars were fixated on the sax, glancing at every inch of its design. I looked downward again and finally folded the neatly typed letter and inserted it back into the envelope. Mr. Jackson and Joshua's names kept circling in my head. *That is phenomenal. If he only knew that Mr. Jackson is my great-great-great grandfather. This is special. Wow!* I, then, stood up, after laying the letter on the table, and put the packing materials away.

Next, I went and picked up three more boxes from off the floor. Surprisingly, I pulled out a second saxophone and then a third one, which were shipped from Pop. Just as the first one, they were in a showcase, too. I chuckled spotting MOSES and DAVID engraved in the same locations.

In the fourth box, I pulled out another one, which was from the queen of my family. It had been engraved, also, as the others with one exception. This one read GRANDFATHER CLOCK followed by CHIMED RIGHT ON TIME. Elated, I stared at all four, side by side, still in their showcases. *Four saxophones?* I probably wouldn't be playing them all. However, a splendid idea hit me. Picking up each one, I took them into another room and came back.

There were now only two more items left on the floor. As I reached for the first one, I scanned the sender's name. Baffled, I wondered what else Nan Mother could possibly have sent me. Much lighter, I opened it in the middle of the floor. *Hmmm, what's this?* I couldn't seem to unroll it fast enough, but, when I did, I immediately smiled, yet, in a state of shock. "Absolutely incredible..." It was a poster of Joshua playing Goldie at Ruby's. Instantly, something dawned on me. *Is that really Goldie?* Observing every inch of the poster, I searched for clues to verify my initial thought. So far, everything appeared just as it should have, except for two things. Looking very closely, I zoned in on the saxophone's case, which lay wide opened on the floor. The lining was a different color. Neither coins nor dollar bills had been tossed everywhere inside, as in the dream. *That's right*, I remembered. *He did have his own saxophone.* When I looked, again, at the sax he had in his hands, I realized it wasn't Goldie after all. Charmed by the black and white poster, I felt in tune to whatever rhythm he played. From what I could see, his stance and expression were deeply rooted by his emotions. Observing how involved he was in completing his mission, I was mesmerized. I wondered what exactly had bolted through his magical fingers. A person, who played like he had twenty fingers, as Ms. PeggyAnn described his capabilities, was seriously "pushing keys to the metal." Coming from her, that was a very strong statement, which was a rewarding compliment. Enthralled, I glanced at the poster, once more, and then stretched it on the floor by placing a small book on each corner to later measure its size for framing.

"All right," I mumbled, anxiously, picking up the last item of suspense. "What do we have here?" Flipping the odd-shaped tube, my eyebrows queried. *Humph. Something else from Mom and Pop?* I ripped it open, reached, and pulled the items out. When I began unrolling one of them, I smiled, immediately staring in the face of GFC. *John Zachariah Alexander—the pendulum of music.* "Umph," I lowly uttered, intensely observing a very important person. *Exactly the man I remember.* There he sat on the edge of a stool with a sax off to the side, resting on a stand. *So, this is the "magnificent" singer, too. Wow!*

Curious now about the other one they'd sent, I laid out GFC's next to the other poster on the floor. My eyes bulged as I unrolled the next one. *"Whaaaaaat..."* The more I unrolled it, the more I recognized. It was so large that I had to place it on the floor, too. Just as the others, I would have never imagined that these even existed—not this many years later. Under examination, the Electric Keynotes were standing together, each with a sax in their hands. Grinning, I shook my head, completely stunned. As I analyzed it more, I was almost positive the black and white snapshot had been taken at the same location as in the dream. They appeared to be wearing, incidentally, the same electrifying suits they had worn that day. I chuckled then laughed out. The more I thought about it, the funnier it became. All I could visualize, at the moment, was when they confused me on stage, rattling off their names consecutively. They sounded as if they had practiced their lines to perfection. Just from that clipping, alone, I couldn't help but laugh out, again. And this time I had to sit down for a few minutes and recoup. I cried.

As soon as I stood up, the doorbell rang. "Whew," was my reaction, blowing out the anticipated rush of air from all the surprises and emotional escalations. I looked out the window, then headed toward the door, while removing shipping items that were in my path. When I opened it, there stood Jarvis with Jordache attached to a leash. Glad to see some familiar faces I hadn't seen since before I'd left for Atlanta, I said, "Hey, Jarvis!"

He grinned. "Devin the man! How are you doing, bruh?!"

Jordache began to pace.

"Fine, my friend. And yourself?"

"I'm doing all right."

This time, she barked.

"Hey, Jordache!" I laughed, "What's going on, girl?!" I stepped outdoors and patted her on the head.

She barked, again, bouncing.

Jarvis chuckled, "I guess she's glad to be back."

I agreed. "She's making it loud and clear."

"Maybe, I should give you the leash before she gets her feet tangled."

I reached for it. "Hold on for a second. She can't go indoors—I have too much lying around inside."

"Sure. Go ahead. Take your time."

Returning in less than a minute, I told him, "Thanks for keeping her for me. I really appreciate it."

"No problem. Delighted to offer. Besides, Sable enjoyed the company."

"I thought she would. They get along very well."

"And that's a good thing."

"It sure is." I opened the door. "Come on in. There's something I want to show you."

Jarvis pushed his cap back. "All right."

"Would you like something to drink?"

He smiled. "That sounds good."

We both washed our hands, chatting all the while, and made our way back toward the kitchen. I opened the refrigerator and handed him one of his favorites. After indulging in a few swallows of Pepsi, I showed him the four showcases in the other room first, then gave him a more in-depth history about the posters that were spread out on the floor.

Amazed by all the evidence, Jarvis said, impressed, "So, this is what you were trying to get me to understand?"

I nodded. "I know it's hard to believe, but here it is."

"From bits and pieces, I had no idea. Some things, I just couldn't visualize." He slowly observed one poster after the next. "This is special. You got something here."

"Definitely," my mind ticked. I had a plan and could clearly visualize the outcome.

"Do you know what you're going to do with your collection?"

"I have an idea, and I'll share that with you later. But first," I decided to say, ready to change the subject since something else percolated, "how is everything coming along? The upcoming event?" I couldn't wait to seize the moment.

He smiled, preparing to turn up his cold drink to down another swig, and said "If Camille only knew…"

...a cherishable moment...

TRUMPET

Much as a grand entrance,
trumpets are classy,
glitzy,
funnel-shaped instruments,
noted for their special deliveries,
a finale.

Its tonal quality,
on demand,
sinks its teeth,
like quicksand,
in a sea of tones,
clinching its wreath,
custom wedding bands,
grinning with glowin',
famous pearly whites.

Through the lips of its passage,
each note is lit,
forcefully with might,
tailored,
parachuting in flight,
beautifully landing,
shining brightly,
relishing,
an unforgettable bliss,
rosy mist.

…sharp, crisp, and profound.

Chapter 19

CAMILLE

Six months later

So many family and friends came to join us for this special occasion. Today marked the beginning—much like a grand entrance. It couldn't have been more real as the tonal qualities of a trumpet rang out inside the walls of a lovely church. Noted for its special deliveries, the trumpet seeped into my meditation. Its tone was so crystal clear and distinct that it had a stronghold on my complete attention. Striking how, through the lips of its passage, the notes were forcefully lit with might. Each parachuted in flight and reached my tender soul. From the thunder, they beautifully and softly landed, shining brightly, turning on faucets of joy. Pronounced, it had been tailored to fit the occasion. The musician beautifully crafted some of life's most beautiful mosaics. Being taken by what followed was just as captivating. In intervals, commanding notes soared and sank their teeth, like quicksand, into a sea of tones that quivered my thoughts. When it clinched its wreath of colorful sounds, as if shaping a profound message into custom wedding bands—just as love interlocked our season—faucets of joy ran over. The height of music kept grinning with glowin', famous pearly whites. Too powerful not to relish, I savored the unforgettable bliss, just as if I had yielded to smell a rosy mist. As a sendoff of the finale, the musician sprinkled notes of salutation. Then, silence. Soon after, the last note sailed, as if drifting off to sleep. Somewhere, beyond every stained window, they were cradled up by beams of light.

After a brief pause came the next segment. Music trailed, floating gently in the air. As expected, Teddy laced nothing but trimmings of eloquence in the rhythm he played. Every note seemed to whisper each second, as a timer, helping with the pace of our steps. As Devin began singing the most beautiful song on our wedding day, as Jarvis and I marched up the red carpet aisle, special moments were captured. Joyous as it should be, smiling faces softly beamed. Passing aisle after aisle, they glowed in an assortment of rainbows. With a mixture of surprise and well wishes, the looks on the faces of Kathy, Paula, and Nancy said a million words. They never suspected that there had been a wedding in the making. And that was how I had wanted it to be since I was the last. Out of all the expressions I had ever seen come across their faces, at that very moment, had to be the best. They graced me well.

Not far away stood Nan Mother, Marcella, Jay, and Josie. How could I ever forget Nan Mother's expression when I shared with her that she was the only one who knew? Between her and my other lady friends, that is. She came, just as she had promised. These memories were for keeps, even something as perplex as the connection between Nan Mother and Devin. The music that we strolled up the aisle to reminded me of the mystery that eventually played. When Maestro returned to California from his trip to Atlanta, he unraveled the suspense of the missing links. Those hidden pieces were colorful as I listened to him explain about the special footage of special people, note by note, who had affected his life. The very first tone of suspense was that I had met Nan Mother. It had been the beginning of something unique and had ended on a good note. Just as how I'd thought it would happen, the unknown had been displayed all in a musical array. The connection was clear, and Nan Mother had played a significant role. She was the catalyst that had not only affected Devin's life but also others, including myself. The outcome was just as fascinating as Teddy's playing at that very moment. As I packaged every memory for keeps with a beautiful bow in my heart, I was swept by a humble voice. I could only smile widely when I saw my Little De standing near Devin. While I was packaging my memories, he had joined Devin chiming in with an amazing but creative voice. I couldn't believe my ears. He sounded well-seasoned, as though he had been chanting the scales of music for years. Handsomely dressed in black, he smiled back. Maestro had hinted around to me that he really wanted for De to be involved, but I had no idea in what capacity. When it came to Little De, I didn't mind. Besides, I knew, whatever Devin suggested, would be favored. He knew well what he did best better than I did. Their surprise could not have been timelier. Tickled within, I realized that I wasn't the only one harboring a well-kept secret.

Reaching the minister, we turned to face him, and he began the ceremony. "We are gathered here today…"

I glanced at my parents and my sister Charla, who were beaming brightly just as Jarvis's parents were. Not far from them, I spotted his two brothers, who were definitely kinsmen. Shadows of evidence spread across their faces with smiles. *Both families have finally come together*, the thought scrolled. I, then, stole a glimpse at the charm beside me. Apparently, he knew I had looked his way; he smiled and took his observation seriously. The minister lightly chuckled and continued.

After all vows were exchanged, it wasn't long after that he finally pronounced our legal union.

Flashes were brightly igniting from all angles as Jarvis and I stood near a large, beautiful, picturesque stained-glass window. From the light of day, the colors glowed. They set off an appealing tint on the adjacent wall, complimenting the inside décor. Seemingly, the silhouette smiled at its own reflection. And so did my sibling and I. Contagiously, Charla and I embraced, smiling just the same at one another's reflection as she congratulated us. As twins, we shared the same etchings in likeness. Jarvis never could seem to get over the similarities.

He chuckled. "Are you pretending to be my wife?" he comically said to me. Jarvis glanced at us both as he had when he'd first met Charla.

Humored by his unexpected statement, we laughed.

Devin and Teddy walked up.

"It's the twins, again," Devin grinned.

"Who is who?" Teddy chimed in, trying to be inconspicuous with so many visitors around. "That is my question."

"I'm trying to figure out if this is my wife? She better be," Jarvis snickered, kissing my forehead.

Laugher ignited, again. I couldn't blame him. Although Charla and I resembled each other a lot, we knew the differences that others couldn't immediately detect.

"It is I," I confirmed, still tickled.

Jarvis ended the charade and admitted, "I know exactly whose finger I put the ring on."

"Man," Devin took it up a notch, "I'm glad you did before you curled up like shrimps."

Teddy chuckled. "Umph." He couldn't say another word.

Neither could Jarvis. Rather, he let it rest then looked at Charla. "Thank you, sis," he finally welcomed her with opened arms. Her eyes were still glassy.

Devin and Teddy gave their well wishes and moved on as another trail of guests approached. When I realized who came behind all the rest, I smiled as widely as they did.

"This day has finally come," Nan Mother brightly said, dressed in a cranberry-colored suit that complimented her crown of glory. Her matching hat could not hide the beauty that it held.

"Yes, it has," I hugged her, "and I'm glad that you're here. Thank you for your presence, Nan Mother. I had hoped that nothing would hinder you from coming."

"Things do happen, but, if I could help it, I wouldn't have missed it for anything." She beamed, then glanced at Jarvis. "You're the gentleman that I envisioned. I know that you are a good man. Take care of my Camille. She's a special lady."

"Thank you, and I will. This is the best Thanksgiving and birthday gift I could ever want. She's my Almond Joy. My prayer went up, and the blessings came down."

Nan Mother nodded with great satisfaction. "I like your language," she smiled at him. "The rhythm of your speech will take you a long ways." Her eyes danced the whole while.

"I know the language you speak of. Only the Man Upstairs is capable of doing that."

She seemed to have jotted an additional assessment of him deep into her mind. "Um…hmmm. This gets better and better," were the last words she said softly.

She gracefully strolled onward, slowly, as Marcella and Josie stepped forward and said a few kind words. Delighted to see them, I embraced them both. As I watched them walk away, in an instant, my mind reflected on the trio back in

Atlanta, who I had had the pleasure of meeting. They were now family.

Just as that thought vanished, Jarvis barely chuckled. "I like that lady." His eyes focused on Nan Mother.

"I thought you would. I don't know of anyone who doesn't find her likeable."

Out of nowhere, De and Jay appeared as another crowd followed. They had the biggest smiles.

I couldn't stop shaking my head.

Jarvis greeted them first, "Fellas."

"De," I hugged him, then Jay. "You were great!"

Jarvis shook hands but patted De on the shoulders twice. "I have to agree with Camille. I had no idea Larry had a son who could sound as you did."

Jay nudged his pal. "Are you convinced now?"

"All right, man. You win."

"You're the man."

"That accolade rings a bell," Jarvis chuckled. "Sounds like something I have said many times. But Jay's right! You manned up today."

For a moment, De seemed a little lost for words. Then, he said, "Thank you, Mr. and Mrs. Brooks." He probably had not expected this much attention.

Jarvis softly tapped him on the arm. "Now, that has a nice ring to it."

The two youngsters glanced at each other and grinned. They did not have time to respond as another crowd ambushed us and then another. And, by the time the last guest had moved on, Kathy and Paula appeared just when the coast was clear. When they spotted us, they wasted no time.

Ecstatically, Paula said, while batting her eyes, still in disbelief, and observing me from head to toe, "Camille, I just cannot believe it." She, then, shook her head swiftly. "You look beautiful. Congratulations to you both."

"Thank you," Jarvis and I replied.

Kathy couldn't wait to edge in, "You have my congrats, too. You both look great."

"Yes, you do," Nancy chimed in, calmly spoken, as she and Larry walked up, smiling. "You look fabulous. Give me a hug, girl."

Larry shook hands and acknowledged everyone else.

Nancy added, "We wish you two the best. You deserve it."

"Jarvis," her husband swiftly said, "I told Nancy this morning that she needed to put on something very nice because we were going to a very special ceremony. I let her know that our presence was requested and we had to be here before one o'clock."

Nancy cut in. "He never let on. I replied," she distinctively but calmly projected her response, giving us a clear picture of how caught off guard she must have been, " 'A ceremony? What kind of ceremony?' " She stared at Larry as if she couldn't believe how well he had kept the secret hidden from her.

"I told her we were going to a wedding."

Further reenacting their conversation, she then said, "My reaction was, 'A wedding? Who's getting married?' " Her unusual animation made us all laugh.

So much expression laid beyond the character of Larry's eyebrows. They rose as if to speak themselves. With humor trailing in his voice, he specifically looked at Jarvis. "Friend, it wasn't easy trying to convince my wife at ten o'clock this morning that you and Camille were scheduled to walk down the aisle and say '*I do.*' " He kept the laughter going. I don't know who was funnier—Nancy or Larry. With full steam, they both captured the moment. He continued his version, "She didn't believe it until we actually drove up in front of the church. Realization set in when she seen all those vehicles parked. She didn't have a clue."

"Neither did we," Paula quickly said as all eyes shifted on her. "Kathy and I received a call from Camille at ten o'clock. She told me to go to the front desk and pick up a special invitation as soon as possible."

"When Paula came back to the room," Kathy energetically said with excitement in her eyes as she stole the moment to finish the story, "she couldn't say a word. It took her a minute to drop the bombshell. We both were baffled. When it finally sunk in, we were ecstatically overcome with joy."

All the energy and heartfelt annotations that leaped from their memories gave me a deep sense of just how much this unexpected celebration had really affected them. Jarvis and I spoke up at the same time. Instead, he decided to let me speak first.

"I can just imagine the reactions, but I wanted to surprise you. All I can say is…thank you for coming. And there's more to come…"

All eyes shifted on Jarvis.

Strangely, he coolly laughed. "If you only knew…"

...what a joyous beat...

REMIX

Remixing parts,
a blending art,
beats,
bleeds,
from the original piece,
hanging in the heart.

Re-creations,
imagination,
new ideas,
animation,
smooth moves,
rolling,
right off the reel,
blindfold.

In seclusion,
music ticked—
notes exchanged,
tones arranged,
in the mix,
synchronizing,
molds that gleamed,
royally,
lustrous,
velvety,
the art...their melody.

...ASCEND...

Chapter 20

DEVIN

"HAPPY BIRTHDAY, JARVIS," voices rang out in an outburst, then slowly sang, *"and wed...ding...daaaaay!"* The crowd dispersed into two separate groups as Josie and Joy became the center focus, *"It is the day that belongs to youuuuuu-oooooo. Happy Birthdaaaay...to youuuuuuu."*

While looking at the expression on Jarvis's face, my guests laughed. Camille's idea of sharing the evening with family and friends in a special way had come as a surprise. Since I had a plan of my own in the making, the timing was perfect. Besides, for someone who had been like a brother to me, I immediately welcomed having the after-five gathering at my home. We were family.

Jarvis smiled. "I knew something was going on, but my wife here wouldn't bulge." He scanned the placed, seemingly looking for someone. When he spotted his suspects, he then pointed at Larry and me. "And you knew all along?"

We chuckled and pointed back at him. "We knew," we both admitted, and most of all, were delighted to be a part of this special evening of extended fellowshipping in just a good-ol'-fashioned kind of way. Larry and I had held our breaths for months, so as not to leak out any information. Our only conversations about this event had only been with Camille. She had it all mapped out, but she wasn't the only one.

The groom looked at Camille as if he was amazed that she had pulled this off and kept her plan so well hidden. His expression turned heartwarming for a lady who had more qualities than he realized. He turned and hugged her.

Taken by sudden emotions, some clapped as others uttered sentiments of joy.

Camille immediately said, "Are there any anniversaries approaching?"

No other couple, other than Larry and Nancy, acknowledged. To everyone else's surprise, he faced her and said, as I signaled De to turn up the microphone, which had been clipped to his lapel, "Happy Anniversary, sweetheart." To be in on his parents' special moment, I showed De what to do. The theatre was nicely lit but somewhat dim. Even so, I noticed the immediate chatter that commenced between Kathy and Paula. They were gleefully transfixed.

Nancy smiled. "Happy Anniversary to you, too, Larry."

He reached inside his jacket and handed her an envelope. "Open it."

When she did, Nancy pulled out some plane tickets. Her mouth unlatched.

"I thought you would say that," he couldn't resist saying.

Everyone laughed. As of yet, Nancy hadn't been able to say one word. Her expression spoke loudly and clearly. The magic word raced from her mouth when she spotted the destination. "Africa."

"Africa!" we heard their son say from the control switch.

Larry grinned widely from their responses. "Yes, Africa. Thank you for the many years that you have stuck by me and for being the lovely wife that you are—"

"Goodness, gracious…it gets better and better," a familiar voice said, walking through the door at the right time with Marcella accompanying her. Nothing but pure sweetness trailed in her voice.

All eyes gazed toward her direction.

Dr. Johnston's upbeat spirit stung those who did not know her and, without a doubt, took the affair up another notch. She had everyone's undivided attention and added, "This is the place for me to be this evening. A place is not a home without love in it; neither is it when love turns dormant in the heart. Larry, I've known you and Nancy for some years," she walked up to them with the kindest smile. "You are a good man, and you have an outstanding wife. In just a few seconds, you have said a trillion words that have not fallen on deaf ears. Imagine a trillion words daily," she emphasized almost to a striking whisper. No matter how close to a whisper she spoke, every word seemed to have swallowed silence. The microphone on Larry's lapel absorbed the dynamics of her speech. "Keep love and truth alive," she sprayed across the room with sincerity, looking around. The mist of inspiration seemed to have taken most by surprise. "Pardon me. I didn't come here to say all that I have said but, being a pediatrician for some years can only humble a person. I know what a trillion words can mean in one breath. A wealth of love is pure gold. Nothing can replace it, but much can take it. Remember…it sets the pace for all things. Our worlds can't go round, peacefully, without it." She headed my way. Then she turned and said one other thing, "Pardon me, again, for not introducing myself first. I'm Nan Mother." She walked on seemingly to be a little tickled in her own world.

Camille immediately said, loud enough for everyone to hear as she and Jarvis approached her, "Thank you, Nan Mother, and thank you for coming. It's been a long day, but you still came anyway."

Jarvis got my attention, giving me the signal. Those who knew the customary routine whenever I raised my hand in the air said in unison, "Thank you, Nan Mother!" For those to jump on board and follow suit, I raised my hand in the air a second time, "THANK YOU, NAN MOTHER!!!" This time, voices roared then collapsed into laughter, including Dr. Johnston.

She shook her head. "Lawd, Lawd, Lawd, this gets better and better..."

Swarmed, she became an instant celebrity.

Immediately, music began to play, softly, in the background.

Jarvis said a few words to Dr. Johnston, then came my way. "I'll take apple juice," he jokingly said.

"That's as good as it gets," I replied.

"I'm with you on that. Besides, we got the best treat of the evening, wouldn't you say?"

"Absolutely, my friend. She even had me thinking."

Jarvis grinned, coolly scanning the place.

"By the way, did you notice the dreamy look on Camille's face when Larry verified that they were going to Africa for their wedding anniversary?"

We moved further away from the crowds to continue the conversation. Jarvis's plan was strictly confidential. The last person he wanted to get a hold of this news was his wife.

He nodded his head. "I saw that. If she only knew. It's hard not telling her, but she'll find out soon enough. While we're in Italy, I'll let her know then. She has three weeks opened; she'll be surprised. There won't be a dull moment for anyone."

"Not a chance. With a party of twelve? There's nothing like family and friends."

"That will be an experience for everyone plus the band. Are you ready for the performance in two weeks?"

"I am. We all need inspiration."

He agreed. "Can't live without it. They'll enjoy it. I'm confident of that. But, bruh," his eyes traveled to where Camille stood, "I must get back to the bride. We'll talk later."

"All right. I'll catch you later."

Apparently, I was the person "chief" was looking for when Pops flagged me down with queen at his side. While I was headed in their direction, Jay stopped me.

"Maestro," he glistened, "that talk we had back in Atlanta several months ago paid off. Thanks, man." Jay tapped my arm.

Momentarily, I couldn't seem to get a grip fast enough on what he was thanking me for, so I asked, "Excuse me for asking but, can you be more specific?" It suddenly dawned on me about our isolated conversation. My mind zoomed back to our one-on-one chat out on Dr. Johnston's patio.

Before I could respond, he replied, "We talked about De. Remember?"

"Yes, I do," I nodded. "You specifically expressed your concern about his low self-esteem, regarding his voice."

Electrified, Jay, then, said, "I knew De could do it. He had a lot of people fooled. As much as we joke around, I've probably heard more than anyone else ever has on a serious note. Thanks." Looking out for Little De meant a lot to him. And he was right! De had even fooled me and reminded me so much of myself growing up. It never dawned on me until now that we had more similarities than originally thought—in more ways than one.

"It's my pleasure. Remember that poem your great-grandfather wrote?"

He smiled.

"You knew De had a hidden chest of jewels. His low self-esteem wouldn't allow them to sparkle." I grinned. "You have inspired him in a clever way." I tapped him on the arm. "And I should be thanking you."

Confusion covered his face. "Thanking me?"

"For bringing out the best in others. And that includes me."

"How?" his eyebrows now queried.

"Soon, you'll see. Now…what about you is the next question?"

"I'm ready."

"That's the spirit."

"So, I guess I better get movin'."

"All right," I replied as Jay briskly made his exit.

The coast was clear. Before anyone else stopped me, I headed, again, toward my parents. They were at a table, getting a glass each of something to drink. I approached them just as they turned and looked up.

"Did you get a chance to greet the mystery lady over there?" My eyes danced in Dr. Johnston's direction.

Mom spoke up first. "Yes, we did. Very nice lady."

"Interesting individual," was Pop's description of her. "Does she know about the relation?"

"Not yet, but she soon will."

"Devin," Mom began to say with plenty of astonishment in her voice, "we love this setup here."

"I didn't want to say anything before you got here, but I thought turning the theatre into a museum would, also, be a good place to display all the items you've sent besides what Nan Mother has personally given and forwarded to me. You know the other sax that had been missing?"

They quickly nodded to hear what I had to say.

"Her husband, Joshua, had it. Paul had given it to him, and Joshua passed it on to me."

The expression on their faces said it all. They found it hard to believe.

"That's amazing and so ironic. It's unbelievable," the words came pouring out of Pop's mouth.

A sudden rush washed over me. "I'm definitely with you on that one." Just the thought warranted me to turn and get something to drink, too.

"Either way you look at it," Mom said, "it's a powerful story."

Dr. Johnston appeared several steps away as I turned back around.

Pop cleared his throat. He said as a way of politely dismissing their presence, "We're going to take another look around this museum of yours."

I nodded.

They casually walked away.

Finally approaching, she smiled. "This has been a lovely day. Picture perfect."

"That it is," I agreed, bubbling inside, as I gazed at the historic trophy standing in front of me, and then asked, "Would you like something to drink or eat, Nan Mother?"

"Sure, water would be fine for now."

I reached for a glass and poured water over the ice. It crackled as I handed it to her. "Let's take a little walk. Shall we?"

She gleamed taking a sip, first. "That would be great."

We walked arm and arm. She had no idea where we were off to.

Once I guided her to Exhibit #1, she realized her surroundings. Dr. Johnston had been detained in conversations ever since she'd made her entrance. Standing side by side, we were now observing the large poster of the Electric Keynotes and their golden brass saxophones. All three in a row were sparkling inside each showcase.

I sat my glass down and reached for hers before she dropped it. She raised her hand to her mouth in awe. Totally mesmerized.

"See this sax?" I pointed. "Your husband passed that one on to me. That is Paul Jackson's saxophone. The box you gave me is what was inside."

"My Joshua said that you are gifted and versatile and would do well. He told me to tell you so. You deserved it, and you do," she now smiled.

"Thank you."

"But that poster," she continued, fascinated, "brings back so many memories. Where did you get it?"

An open window presented itself. She asked a question I knew would soon come. "From my parents. And I know you're wondering where they could have gotten it."

Intrigued, she waited for a replied. Her stare was as if she searched the regions of my mind to get a peek inside.

I told her the most explosive information yet, "To my surprise, Nan Mother, the Electric Keynotes are my great-great-great-grandfathers."

Her eyes inflated. "What!" she said as if she had seen a ghost.

"Yes," I reiterated and swiftly took her to the next exhibit of Grandfather Clock, since what came next would be just as jarring. I continued the presentation, "This is my…great-great-grandfather." The poster of him and his sax were a striking pair.

She gasped. "Oh, dear. *All of them are related to you?*"

I nodded still in disbelief. "I couldn't believe it either."

Speechless, she couldn't get a word out. Under the circumstances, I kept a straight face and moved on to the remaining exhibits. When we reached the next one, I smiled, raising my hand toward the poster of Joshua playing his saxophone at Ruby's. His black hat was displayed in a showcase, underneath, on a tall pedestal.

"The musician and poet," were my entertaining words.

She unleashed another big smile and touched the edge of the case. The word INSPIRED, sparkling on the hat, seemed to have captivated us. It had affected both our lives.

"Umph, umph, umph…my diamond ring," she said as if still amazed. For the moment, her thoughts were taken elsewhere.

Jay walked up from behind. "Excuse me, but, Nan Mother, you left this in the car." He handed it to her and left.

"Oh, yes." She handed it to me. "Idella's husband, Reginald, contacted me and wondered if I had a copy of this drawing that his wife had drawn. I'm sending him the original that PeggyAnn sketched, which he preferred to have as a surprise for his wife; and, I had an extra copy made for you, which has her signature on it. Since you were so drawn to it, you'll always have something to remember Josephine and me. And, especially PeggyAnn since, she's the originator."

"Perfect," I smiled and observed what seemed like an unusual artifact. Due to its history, it was. "Thank you. I'll put it on display as well."

"You are welcome."

To my surprise, she added, while staring at the drawing, what I had assumed would never resurface again, "Around the time PeggyAnn sketched that drawing is when I learned we, possibly, were leaving Oklahoma for good. I had family and friends there I didn't want to leave. I never told my parents my true feelings. Eventually, I did, but it wasn't until after PeggyAnn, Joshua, and Josephine paid me a visit. And it wasn't until Joshua and I married that I learned that my father had requested that they stop by."

Recapturing moments of the 1920s, again, brought her happiness from way deep inside the greenery of her thoughts. I refrained from interrupting her; I just wanted her to speak since I knew how much it meant to her.

She slightly chuckled and finally looked up and gazed at me. Almost at a whisper, I barely heard her say, "Things happened in the strangest way."

Without raising any suspicion, I limited my response as I agreed emphatically, "I'm a witness, and I can attest to that."

On that note, we moved along to the last exhibit. There, I posed in a photograph with Mr. Jackson's saxophone. Joshua's letter had been framed underneath. "Nan Mother," I pointed at the frame, "that letter is from your husband. You're welcome to read it."

She walked to it and read it entirely. Staring, she couldn't seem to take her eyes off it. Then, she gazed at the picture, again, and said, "It's almost as if he knew..." Her gaze fell on me.

Baffled, I asked, "Knew?"

"Of your relation to the Jackson family."

On target, I had to agree with her inclination, "Exactly my thought when I learned of the news. Somehow, I got that same feeling, Nan Mother."

"And he sure would've been surprised about your connection to Mr. Alexander."

"You're right. Just as all the rest of us."

"Lawd—"

"This gets better and better," I chirped and smiled, finishing the sentence for her.

Tickled, she patted my arm. I couldn't resist reciting her famous words. If I had a difficult time remembering anything else special about her, I would never forget that.

"Now, I understand," she paused, "why this weekend was so important."

"I wouldn't have wished it any other way," I proclaimed.

"Likewise. Life sure has a way of snowing beautifully like rain."

"And casting spells. Wouldn't you say?" I chuckled.

"Well...yes, and in the most unexpected way." Dr. Johnston then shook her head, mildly, "Jo-Jo sure has a striking way of reaching her audience. It's almost as if she knew, too." She looked up toward me in astonishment. "Eyes of the melody have been staring me in the face since the day," she shook her head, again, "we met."

"Eyes of the melody?"

"Yes. Do you remember the song we were listening to at my home?"

"Oh," I grinned, "those eyes."

She nodded. "You are the link to such an amazing revelation."

Understanding the logic of how she felt, I added fervently, "The wings of the melody are opened wide. What we didn't know is no longer hidden."

"It certainly isn't, Maestro. The snow is stunning in full bloom."

"I like that," I responded as I turned to glance, once more, at each item on exhibition.

She looked in the same direction.

"The keynotes of each of these icons will swing in my consciousness for life. Sweetsations—"

Edging in with grace, she stated, "Sweetsations of joy. Am I right?"

"Yes, and that includes you, Nan Mother. I can't forget about you, and I definitely can't forget about him," I pointed as I turned in the opposite direction.

With endearment, she smiled. "You're so kind," was all she could say for the moment.

For a second time, we were drawn to observe the poster of Joshua at Ruby's. The same thought that surfaced many times before flashed in my head. "I'm curious as to what he played that day." His stance captivated me.

Before Dr. Johnston could reply, the sound of live music engulfed the theatre.

As if hypnotized, she turned slowly.

Little Joshua stole the moment.

We both faced the direction in which the music spiraled from. A smile sweetly crept across her face. Passionate about what she had heard, she was swept away.

"That's interesting that you've asked," Dr. Johnston stared straight ahead. "Jay is playing it as we speak."

I gently smiled. *It wasn't the same music I played at Ruby's after all.* Completely shocked, I could see, in plain view, that same poem from the dream lying inside Jay's saxophone case. It appeared fresh off the press. Apparently, it was a tradition. And I understood why. "That was part of your future engagement?" I looked below for the signature of her admission.

She briefly looked upward. As proof, the answer to my question was pleasantly scribbled across her face. "Yes, it certainly was. Papa Jay taught him years ago. It's been a long time since I heard my great-grandson play. I can't believe how much that sounds like—"

"The man who played like he had twenty fingers?" I purposely cut in to humor her.

Question marks were dangling in her eyes like dollar signs. I guess that was a million dollar question. She probably wondered how I knew. Rather than ask, she beamed and slightly laughed, then told me one other missing piece of the puzzle. "How could I ever forget?" her eyes sparkled. "That's also the same music Joshua played at my parents' home the day PeggyAnn drew that sketch of Josephine and I."

Only one word dropped from off the cliff of my brain, "Unbelievable."

"Maestro, I feel the same way. That's a lovely song." She looked on as others who were enthralled.

Marcella and Josie walked up behind De, engrossed by Jay's performance.

"Isn't he great?" Camille said, impressed as she and Jarvis joined us. Engaged, we just let her comment simmer in our flowing thoughts as we sailed. Confirmation was evident.

Lasting imageries of Jay were ingrained for a lifetime. Whether he realized it or not, he played a very important role that took place in history. Finally, the remaining pieces of the puzzle had been revealed. There was no more film left reflecting on the past; the reel had stopped. And maybe this time...*for good*.

The evening began to slowly shut its eyes, but, before the affair came to a close, there was one last thing I had to do. I reached for the sax and locked the showcase. Then, I walked near the stool and placed the shiny apparatus on the stand and took off my jacket. The lights dimmed. After clipping the neckpiece, I stood beside the big screen as I heard the sound of my own voice rip through the speakers in the theatre. While closing the evening affair with Goldie in my hands, I tuned in to what was displayed on-screen. From deep within, I could hear Moses' advice, tapping in along the seashore of my mind, saying, "Young man, capture your niche." With that thought, in full swing, I could only play music from the rhythm displayed in my sky. As I played calligraphies of notes, one behind the other, I wanted to let the Man Upstairs know that His Ribbons of love, joy, and peace for all humankind came straight from the heart. And they were all colorful to sail across anyone's horizon.

At a snail's pace, segments of what I played at Ruby's were ticking, solo, at the same time, only in my head. How could I ever forget? Unexpectedly, it turned out to be a remix, a striking combo for me personally. And, for good reasons. Some things could never be expressed fully, in words. In the most appreciative way and by musical expression, I had mastered the blending art, which could only bleed from the original piece that hanged in the heart. Re-creation with a little imagination and new ideas rolled right off the reel, blindfolded. With my eyes closed, the effects of being in seclusion rang distinctively. I could feel the profuse bleeding from the impulse. Signaling my tower, there were times that notes exchanged. Tones were arranged in the mix as molds of historical people, important to me, synchronized and gleamed, royally. I threaded that same purple melody as before with royalty. Satiated by its richness, the dispersion of its contents danced through the brass carving. Goldie sounded silky-rich-and-velvety. Just as I had imagined, I visualized their destinies shining with sheen. Life was like art; it was definitely their melodies.

While reaching the last thunder of rain along the musical tree, as my eyes gradually opened, splashes of tunes covered imprints of those who could never be forgotten. And at the same time, I could only wonder where the sands of time would lead those who filled this same room. I smiled inside as the final power of wavelengths recessed. Even after every wave continuously roared upon the land, clearly along the shoreline of my mind, the depths of historical shoes were still, deeply and broadly imprinted, as far as the eyes could see and beyond. The panoramic view was as beautiful as He had made it. *Fascinating*, that thought quickly streamed from somewhere far away. All I could do, now, was let it ascend. Once I finished, I withdrew from the coastline. Music lingered in my imagination like dew. *Where did the rain go?*

As if the crack of dawn had glowed across the theatre, I awakened out of a musical sleep, seeing Jay nodding his approval. Smiling, my eyes soon landed on the perfect sunshine. Faith stole my immediate attention.

She brightly beamed.

I chuckled, fascinated, thinking, *Could this possibly be part of my own future engagement?*

Jarvis and Camille stood not far from her. He grinned. His observation pierced through the lining of truth.

I chuckled as another purple melody danced on my rooftop. And, the beat goes on...

...CRESCENDO...

PURPLE MELODY

Purple melodies,
glisten like snowflakes,
drizzles,
flurries,
then,
snows as it flows.

How great the sound,
where melodies accumulated,
frosted above the sand of life,
too many for calculation,
an amazing site of tunes,
compressed by its weight,
it's stunning in full bloom.

A purple melody earned its stripes,
by sounds it foretold,
whose melodies they are,
critiqued with brushes of life,
swelled by the colors of its tempos,
growing with gravity in its dimples.

Melodies are sifted,
in tuned to passages of life,
broken down and shifted,
across the scale,
sailing melodically,
delivering its classified mail.

Whose melodies is it?
It snowed like rain,

casting spells,
in the purple dawn,
softly drifting above the plains,
on somebody's land,
in the heart,
a debut,
threaded with royalty,
playing,
Purple Melody.

A Personal Note

On a personal note, this book is also to family and friends who not only love but is passionate about music, whether instrumentally or vocally. There are *too many* names to mention, so, instead I will not make note of anyone, specifically, because, I may miss someone unintentionally. Rather, I will let that thought play in the cabinet of my heart of those who I know to cherish the passport of joyful sounds.

Peace to all,
"Inspire"

About the Author

*P*urple Melody is SANDRA PORTER'S third novel of The Brooks Series. She has, also, written *Whistling in the Wind* and *Reflections in My Tea*. She is a former resident of Phoenix, Arizona and currently resides in Georgia.